RANDOM HOUSE
CHILDREN'S BOOKS
A DIVISION OF RANDOM HOUSE, INC.

TITLE: Solace of the Road
AUTHOR: Siobhan Dowd
IMPRINT: David Fickling Books
PUBLICATION DATE: October 13, 2009
ISBN: 978-0-375-84971-8
PRICE: $17.99 U.S./$22.00 CAN.
GLB ISBN: 978-0-375-94971-5
GLB PRICE: $20.99 U.S./$25.99 CAN.
E-BOOK ISBN: 978-0-375-89365-0
E-BOOK PRICE: $17.99 U.S./$22.00 CAN.
PAGES: 272
AGES: 14 and up

Please send two copies of any review or mention of this book to:
Random House Children's Books Publicity Department
1745 Broadway, Mail Drop 10-1
New York, NY 10019

solace of the road

www.**davidficklingbooks**.co.uk

SIOBHAN DOWD
solace of the road

David Fickling Books

OXFORD · NEW YORK

31 Beaumont Street
Oxford OX1 2NP, UK

SOLACE OF THE ROAD
A DAVID FICKLING BOOK 978 0 385 60971 5

Published in Great Britain by David Fickling Books,
a division of Random House Children's Books
A Random House Group Company

This edition published 2009

1 3 5 7 9 10 8 6 4 2

Copyright © 2009 The Literary Estate of Siobhan Dowd

The right of Siobhan Dowd to be identified as the author of this
work has been asserted in accordance with the Copyright,
Designs and Patents Act 1988.

The Random House Group Limited supports the Forest
Stewardship Council (FSC), the leading international forest
certification organization. All our titles that are printed on
Greenpeace-approved FSC-certified paper carry the FSC logo.
Our paper procurement policy can be found at
www.rbooks.co.uk/environment.

Mixed Sources
Product group from well managed
forests and other controlled sources
FSC   www.fsc.org Cert no. TT-COC-2139
© 1996 Forest Stewardship Council

Set in New Baskerville

DAVID FICKLING BOOKS
31 Beaumont Street, Oxford, OX1 2NP

www.kidsatrandomhouse.co.uk
www.rbooks.co.uk

Addresses for companies within The Random House Group Limited
can be found at: www.randomhouse.co.uk/offices.htm

THE RANDOM HOUSE GROUP Limited Reg. No. 954009

A CIP catalogue record for this book is available from the British Library.

Printed and bound in Great Britain by Clays Ltd, St Ives plc

For Anna

If I was where I would be,
Then I would be where I am not.
Here I am where I must be,
Where I would be, I cannot.

from 'Katie Cruel', a traditional song

One

Fishguard

I breezed down the line of cars, so cool you'd never have known I was looking for a way to board the boat.

I strolled along easy, blonde, the wig catching the light. Then I spotted it. A shiny navy four-by-four, seven-seater and no kids. The owners, grey-haired coat-flappers, had just got out, leaving the front doors wide open. They were metres away, looking out to sea, talking to somebody further up the queue.

They were mogits, one hundred per cent. Mogit's the word Trim, Grace and I made up in Templeton House and it stands for Miserable Old Git.

I glanced in. Coats, magazines, newspapers. A child seat, but no child. Untidy. Perfect. I got in through the passenger door and squeezed into the back.

It smelled of dog hair and plastic, all mixed up. I curled up on the floor and covered myself over with the coats. It was quiet, dark and still. I couldn't hear the wind.

I was off to Ireland under my own steam.

I waited. My skin prickled. My nose twitched. Jeez, agony. *What the hell am I doing here?* It was like I'd jolted awake in the middle of a dream to find I was in the same place and the dream was real. I nearly got up and dashed out but the owners came back. I froze. They got in and the four-by-four shook. That's when the wig slipped. I felt it topple off the side of my head and I couldn't do a thing. I scrunched up my eyes and clenched my teeth. The owners started talking. The car doors banged shut and the engine started.

'About time,' Mr Mogit grumbled. 'We've been hanging around all morning.'

'Your decision to leave at the crack of dawn. Not mine.' (Mrs Mogit.)

'It was my contingency time.'

'You and your contingencies.'

'What about the time the tyre blew?'

'What *about* the time the tyre blew?'

'You were glad we left early then.'

'That was years ago. Before the grandchildren. Before the *children*!'

'So. We're due another contingency any minute.'

'Saints preserve us. Stop gurning. Your man's waving us on.'

I didn't know what they were on about. Con-ten-gin-sea. It sounded like a weirdo cocktail, the kind you'd get at the Clone Zone. They had odd accents, these mogits, not like the other Irish people I knew. Not like Mammy or Denny, the nightmare man. Certainly not like Miko. But I was glad they were arguing, because they didn't turn round. Mr Mogit

2

revved the engine. We crept forward. We must have got to the ticket kiosk because I could hear the ferry officer checking their tickets. Would he spot the bulge on the floor at the back? I felt my luck tiptoeing away. Without the wig on, Solace was gone. I was plain old Holly Hogan again, the girl nobody wanted. But no. A miracle. The car banged over the ramp and there was a boomerang echo. Then voices, doors slamming, metal drumming. And somewhere the ship's engine, deep and hot, turning. Even though I was under the coats, I could feel a strange heat rising and the pipes and the low-slung ceiling looming overhead, like somebody pinning me down the way they did when they locked me in at the secure unit.

I held my breath.

'Don't forget the food,' Mr Mogit called. His voice felt close now we were inside the boat's belly.

'I've got it here at my feet.'

'Great. Parma ham with cheese.'

'Ach, shut it.'

'Can't take a joke.'

'Not after six hours cooped up in here. This journey's been as long as a wet week. Let's get out.'

'Shall we take the coats?'

That's it. Caught.

'It's broiling. It's sunscreen we need.'

Mr Mogit laughed. 'You're something else. Pass the bag over.'

I heard shuffling. The four-by-four shuddered as they got out.

'It's the bowels of hell down here,' Mrs Mogit said. 'Let's go straight up on deck.'

Now or never. They'll give the car a once-over and see me, or they won't.

The front doors slammed shut at the same time. Then something happened that I hadn't bargained for.

KRAAACRUUUNKK.

They'd locked the doors all at once with me inside. Oh, God. I could hear a muffle of voices drifting away.

When you're in a car and somebody's locked it from the outside, can you get out?

If you can't get out, can you open the window?

If you can't open the window, how long can you breathe the air that's in the car? Does it last a crossing of the Irish Sea?

If it runs out before you get to the other side, do you die?

The questions fizzed in my brain like angry bees. I stayed rigid. Doors slammed. People walked by. Once the four-by-four rocked when somebody bumped into it. Then the noises of the cars and people went away. All I could hear was the big hot sound of the boat.

I pushed the coats back from my face and found myself staring up at cream and green flecks on the car ceiling. Then the flecks dissolved and instead I saw the sky house. The sky house is the last place I lived with Mam, way back. The clouds pressed up against the windows. Mammy and Denny were arguing, then they were laughing and the ice in Mam's see-through drink was clicking and I was holding out an empty tube of toothpaste. *No. Not that.* I scrubbed the scene out like chalk from a blackboard. Mam was sitting at the mirror again, in her black dress, the one with the slinky halter-neck. The wind was in her hair even though she was indoors. And I was brushing her hair. *That's better. Don't stop brushing, Holly, for love nor money.* But I was here alone with the cream and green flecks. I felt a hot tear roll down my face. They'd come and gone, the good guys, the bad, the ones who cared and the most who didn't. There was only me left and the hollow *boom-boom* of the ship. I saw my dream of Ireland winking at me, but how can you sail into a dream? Dreams are like mirrors. You walk towards them and a cold pane of glass stops you.

Ireland. Green grass, moving.

Mam singing, *Sweet dreams are made of this.*

Cows going over the hill.

Freedom.

Where dogs laugh, showing their bellies.

And Mam smiles. *Welcome home, love.*

I sat up on the seat, stroking the wig on my lap. The seat leather was grey and soft. My cheeks burned. I breathed. *Calm down, Holl.* I tried the door.

Locked.

I pressed the buttons to scroll down the window. Nothing.

Stay cool, girl.

I peered out. Dim lighting, car on car, lines of bumpers, empty glass, drab colours. Then a lurch and roll. We were moving.

Jeez. Mrs Mogit was right. It was the bowels of hell down here. My stomach tilted, a half-beat behind the rest of me. I banged the windows. I hollered like a trumpet but the swaying didn't stop. The airless heat will pass me out, I thought. *Mammy*, I thought. *You're out there somewhere. On the other side of the glass. Come and get me.*

Let me out. Please. Somebody. Anybody.

Let.

Me.

Out.

The boat rolled. I screamed. I pounded the glass.

The darkness came down like a blanket in my brain. Underneath, the sea yawned. But nobody came.

Two

The Placement Prospect

In the darkness, I was falling backwards to where I'd started my journey. The road I'd taken disappeared from under my feet, the mountains and castles and hills and tarmac crumbled and I was at the beginning again, back to how I left the Home. And that was down to Miko.

'Miko,' I said out loud. 'Miko? Where've you gone?' And there he was, in my mind, smiling at me. Tall as a door, with a mean whisper of hair. He was looking down at me from the top of a hill, his guitar slung over his back. *Hurry, hurry, Holly Hogan*, he sang. It was the tune he made up for me, the time we all went to Devon. *Before the road disappears beneath your feet.* Then he shook his head and turned away and vanished.

Miko was my key worker at Templeton House. That meant I was his special concern. His name was short for Michael and pronounced My-co. He had a unicorn tattoo on his forearm and he could juggle anything: slices of toast, a jam jar and a bunch of keys.

Miko taught me to upend my mattress against the wall and kick it until all the nail-bomb bits in my brain stopped blowing. And though he didn't have an accent, Miko was Irish originally, just like me and just like my mam. I liked him fine. He was on my side.

I was fourteen. I'd been in Templeton House longer than anyone, counting Miko. I'd seen them come and go, the staff and the care-babes both, but I liked it best now Miko was around. Miko helped me paint my room green and white. Over the window he'd hung the gold curtains my friend Grace and I'd found down the indoor market. So my room was green, white and gold, the colours of Ireland, and Ireland was in my room.

My room had all my best things. Drew from Storm Alert, my favourite band, smouldered down with his brown eyes from the wall posters. On the bed was Rosabel, the fluffy toy dog I'd had for ever. Rosabel followed me everywhere when I was little. I fed her bits of dinner and they'd pile up between her paws and go off. Then when Miko came he said, 'Holly, it's getting old.' I was twelve. So I put Rosabel at the foot of the bed and there she stayed, warming my feet, and I stopped pretending she was real.

Most precious of all was Mam's amber ring in my shell box on the shelf.

Templeton House was for six kids – three boys, three girls. The boys slept in the annexe at the back and the girls slept in rooms upstairs. Grace was my favourite girl and Trim my favourite boy. They were a year older than me. Trim's second name was Trouble

8

and Grace's was Gorgeous. Grace, Trim and me went out cruising the tubes most Sundays and sometimes school days too. We were the hairy-scary care-babes and the younger ones stayed out of our way.

Miko said in his reports how I was sliding. I needed to stop letting others lead me off the rails. By 'others', he meant Grace and Trim but he never said so.

Then one day he came into the lounge and said, 'Holly, I've news for you.'

We were watching the *Titanic* sink for the fiftieth time. It was lashing down rain outside and there was nothing else to do. There I was, sprawled on the bean-bag with Grace leaning against my legs so I could sort through her beauty braids. I could hardly keep my eyes open, the rain made me so dreamy. I was imagining I was back in Ireland where it rains all the time. I hadn't been there since I was small but I could see it still. I thought myself onto a green hill with Mam on the top. She was wearing her black halter-neck and her hair was rippling and shining in the wind. And the rain was so soft it was like walking through silk.

We'd got to the bit where Kate W runs to get the axe.

'Shut the fuck up,' Trim raved at Miko. *Titanic* was Trim's all-time favourite film. Munching a crisp was enough to wind Trim up when *Titanic* was playing.

'Yeah, what news, Miko?' I asked, not really interested, and Trim smashed his fist to within an inch of my nose.

Miko jerked his head, meaning 'outside'. So I left Kate W running down the ship's corridor and followed Miko out to the little staff office with all the files. The files were lined up in grey boxes and each person's name was on at least one box, and the longer they'd been in Templeton House the more boxes they had. I had six boxes, more than anyone.

Miko sat on the swivel chair. I sat on a wooden fold-up chair by the window and rested my trainers on the edge of the litterbin. You could see the garden from there and it was grey and brown and dripping, which was fine. I was smiling, thinking how if I was Kate W with the axe I'd have gone for the creepy man who wants to marry her.

'Holly,' Miko said.

'Yeah. What?'

'Do you want to know what's new or not?'

'Whatever.'

'It's a placement prospect, Holly.'

I shrugged. I'd heard that one before. It never came to anything.

'It's just what you wanted. Nice-sounding couple. No kids.'

He was grinning ear to ear like I'd won the lottery. I reached over and got a scrunched-up ball of paper out of the bin and dropped it from one hand into the other.

'You're in *serious* luck, this time,' Miko said.

'Oh, yeah?'

'Honestly. I've chatted it over with Rachel.' Rachel is my social worker, which is different from a key worker. A key worker lives part-time in the Home with you and the social worker just works nine to five in an office, same as anyone.

'She's met them and she thinks they're really good people,' Miko was going.

Good people. I put a finger in my mouth, down my throat.

'OK. *Nice* people. They have a very pretty house. Victorian and all done up. You'd have a room all your own. And like I said, no kids.'

'Are they Irish?' I said.

'Hey?'

'Grace only has black placements. So I only want Irish.'

'C'mon, Holly. Their name's Aldridge. Which isn't very Irish. But most English people have a bit of Irish somewhere – it's a fact.'

'Huh.'

'So?'

'So what?'

'What d'you *think*, Holly?'

I threw the paper ball right at Miko but instead of it hitting him in the nose like I'd intended, he caught it real fast.

'That's what I think,' I said. 'Crap-ville.'

Miko threw the paper ball right back at me and I hit it back and we volleyed it around some and then he headed it straight back into the litterbin.

'Aw, Holly,' he said.

'Aw, Miko,' I said. I couldn't help smiling. Miko was the best footballer I knew not signed up professional. 'I don't want a placement,' I said. 'I like it fine here.'

'But school, Holly. You never go. With the Aldridges you'd start fresh at a new school. A better school.'

I looked as if to say *Throw me another lemon.*

'Holly.' Miko's voice went quiet.

'Yeah?'

'Don't pass this placement up on my account. Will you?'

I got the zipper of my sweatshirt and gave it a yank. 'Ha ha. As if.'

'Because, Holly, there's something I want you to know.'

'Yeah, what?'

'I'm leaving here.'

There was a long silence. I turned back to the window and watched the raindrops cruising down like ants on a doomed mission. 'Leaving?' My voice felt small. 'What d'you mean, leaving?'

'I'm applying for a new job. It's time.'

The rules said that when you and your key worker parted company, that was the end of all contact. For ever.

'But what about our summer plans, Miko? We're going back to Devon again, right? You promised. You're gonna teach us surfing, right? What about those plans, Miko?'

He didn't answer.

'What d'you mean it's time?' I could feel myself losing it.

Then Miko's hand was on my shoulder. 'Oh, Holly.'

'You're my key worker, Miko. You and me. We're a team. You said.'

'It's hard, really hard to explain. See . . .'

I bit my lip.

'I've got to go, Holly. There's nothing much I can do here any more. You're on a slide. Like I keep saying. You need a real home. You deserve a real home. And the Aldridges have one. Just waiting for you. Trust me, Holly.'

I got up from the chair and gripped the hard edge. I didn't want Miko to see my face so I turned back to the window and stared out at the dismal trees.

'And I've got to go for another reason, Holly. It's the shift work. It's ruining my relationship.' He was talking about his girlfriend, Yvette. Up to then I'd never even thought she was real, with a name like that.

' 'S wet out there,' I said.

'Just agree to meet them. Then see how you feel, Holly. Go on. Please.'

I stared at the dead leaves stuck on the lawn. 'Soaking.'

'Is that a yes, Holly?'

I didn't answer.

'Just a yes to meeting them, no strings attached?'

I waved a hand at him. 'Yeah, Miko. Whatever you want. I'm going back to watch all those Irish people in third class get freed.'

And I drifted back to the lounge and the *Titanic* was half in and half out of the water at a bad angle.

Grace was hunched on the floor, starting to paint her toenails a weird colour that the bottle said was called XTC. The room stank like bad deodorant. The room always stank like bad deodorant. Trim was sitting up on the sofa's back and punching the air as the ship went down.

I sat next to Grace. 'Pass the bottle over, Grace. I'll do the rest for you.'

But instead I splattered a load of polish down on the oatmeal carpet like violet sick.

'What d'you do that for, cow-witch?' Grace screeched.

'Shut the fuck up,' Trim raved.

Placement prospect? More like pass the bloody parcel.

Templeton House without Miko? I'd rather have a ticket on the *Titanic* any day.

Three

Goodbye, Templeton House

Ray and Fiona Aldridge lived in a place called Tooting Bec. They came to visit me at the Home the first time we met. Miko showed them up to my bedroom and left us there.

Fiona was small, with a pinched-up face and crow-lines round the eyes. She had a pixie nose and wavy hair, cut into a crooked bob, like she'd tried to do it herself. She wore dangling bell-things in her ears and a chunky jumper with red and green flecks. I read her right off. She was the kind of person who dresses poorer than she is and saves the whales. The kind of person who'd adopt a three-legged dog.

She sat next to me on the bed like we were old mates and spoke posh and soft and real polite. Ray didn't say much. He stood by the door, his eyes off to the side, bored. He was thin and neat.

After the introductions were over, there didn't seem much to say.

Then Fiona asked me when my birthday was.

'What d'you think, name like Holly?' I said.

Fiona smiled. 'It's a nice name. I suppose you came along around Christmas?'

'That's what everyone says. Only my birthday's in June.'

'June? That's a good time. The holly's green all year round, isn't it?'

'Is it?'

'Yes, I think so.'

'What about the berries?'

'The berries? They only come in winter, I suppose.'

Great, I thought. So I'm a holly with no berries, just the prickles. Guess that's when I decided she was another mogit, whatever about the smiles and nods and sitting next to me on the bed.

I don't know why but I picked Rosabel up from my pillow and said how she was my pet dog from Ireland and was she allowed into their house too? Then I made a pretend bark. '*Grrr-rap!*' And Fiona laughed and said she certainly was, any time.

And I don't know why I did this either, but I asked why they didn't have kids. What I really wanted to know was why they wanted me to come home with them. But Fiona said in a sad voice that she couldn't, and she didn't talk about it any more.

They said some more about how their house was by a common and how they had a room ready for me. Then they both shook my hand like I was a business prospect, and left.

After they'd gone, Miko came and asked what I thought.

16

'Mogits,' I said. 'Both of them. One hundred per cent.'

'Aw, Holly,' Miko said. 'Is that all you can say?'

'Yep.'

'Do you want to pursue this or not?'

'Dunno.'

Then he started up again about how it was time I moved on, I'd be better off out of Templeton House, things were getting way too hairy here, and on and on. I scratched my head like I had nits, pretending not to follow. Then he dropped his voice. 'Holly, I've just heard. I've got an interview. For that job. I'm on my way.'

I stared. A cold-bath feeling came down on me. I'd been thinking how maybe Miko wouldn't get the job, end of story, how he'd go on being my key worker and how the Aldridges could take a sky-jump.

The shift work. It's ruining my relationship.

'An interview?' I said. I picked up Rosabel and twirled her by the ear. I thought how maybe the people at the new job wouldn't like him. And then how everybody liked Miko. The job would be his, sure as sunset.

Miko got up. 'Yeah. Next Monday. So think about it, Holly. I've got a feeling about Fiona and Ray. They're a chance in a million for you. You could go for a trial weekend.'

'Oh, yeah?'

'Yes, Holly. What do you think?'

I lay back on the bed and examined Rosabel's brown front paw, imagining I was taking a stone out

17

from her toe-pads. '*Grr-rap!*' I said again. Miko leaned against the doorframe with his head tilted, like he was waiting. So I held Rosabel up and said in a gruff doggy voice, 'OK. We'll give the mogits a go. *Grr-rap.*'

'You serious, Holly?'

'Yeah. Whatever.'

Miko's face lit up like Ireland had won the World Cup.

And that's when I knew I didn't really have a choice.

Four

Hello, Mercutia Road

The day of the trial weekend at Fiona and Ray's, Grace, Trim and I stood in a three-way knot, arms and legs muddled. I felt Grace's smooth cheek and Trim's rude-boy elbows. Miko lounged against the front door of Templeton House and waved. 'Knock 'em dead, Holly,' he called.

As if.

It was Rachel's job to take me on the tube to the Aldridges' house. They lived on a street called Mercutia Road. The trees along it had yellow leaves. It was posh, with big tall houses in old yellow brick, and the kind of windows called sash. They looked down on you, all smug. The purple-grey roofs were the same colour as the sky. The doors were painted different colours. They had fancy door-knockers and slits for mail and seven steps up to them.

'This is it,' Rachel said. 'Number twenty-two.'

'Yeah.'

'How're you feeling, Holly?'

'Fine.'

19

'Not nervous?'

'Nah.'

That first weekend I did everything Fiona said. She suggested I go to bed, I did. I didn't put my earphones in when she was talking to me. I tried not to mind her making conversation all day long like some kind of recorded announcement on the Underground. That's what her voice was like, the woman who tells you to alight here and mind the gap between the train and the platform edge. Posh and phoney.

Like the house. There was wood everywhere, even in the toilet. And everywhere was neat and tidy and just so. I swear I tried not to breathe from Friday to Sunday night.

At least Fiona and Ray had no kids. I'd be free of little brats here, not like in that placement at the Kavanaghs'. The brat there had given me a hard time. The worst thing was how he tore up the only photo I had of my mam. That was like being stabbed in the eye and his mother refused to believe he'd done it.

Here I had my own room and could keep everything private. I had a big bed with an apricot duvet, soft as they come, a chest of drawers with a key and a wardrobe with a long mirror. From the ceiling a lamp with glass pendants hung low, catching the colours in the room. By the window was a glass-topped desk and you could sit and look out over the garden to an ivy wall. Beyond the wall was more yellow brick and smug windows and beyond that the common. Tooting Bec. Snooting Heck.

'Do you like it?' Fiona said. 'We've just had it decorated.'

I thought how at the Home, Miko'd draped the gold lamé curtains I'd chosen, all elegant over the window.

' 'S fine,' I said. I'd brought Rosabel with me and put her on the pillow for a nap.

Fiona asked me what I liked to eat. I told her how I hated eggs. OK, she said. No eggs. Then I said pizza was my favourite and she got it for me.

The second weekend was the same. I went back to the Home on the Sunday night. Ray dropped me. He'd drive the car and say 'Nearly there now' every time he turned a corner. That's how I knew the fostering was Fiona's idea, not his. He couldn't wait to see the back of me.

Come Christmas, Miko and Rachel told me they had a surprise present for me. The Aldridges were ready for me to live there, a proper placement. They liked me fine, Rachel said, and thought I'd fit in.

Yeah, I thought, like a heavy metal singer in a ballet class. 'How long do they want me for?'

'Open ended, Holly. Isn't that great? They're really keen,' Rachel said.

'Open ended? So they can send me back whenever?'

Miko waved a hand. 'Why would they do that, Holly? You're going to go straight, hey?'

Like I was some big-time crook. 'Dunno, Miko. Being delinquent's awful fun.'

Miko raised a brow.

21

'OK, OK, I'll try,' I said. 'But if they send me back, it's not my fault. It means they don't want to know.'

'It's open ended on *both* sides, Holly. You can decide you've had enough too.' Rachel grinned. She was OK, Rachel. Only fifty per cent mogit. Some people, like Grace, have social workers that hardly ever come near you, and when they do they talk like you're trash. Rachel wasn't like that.

So in January, just before school started up, she took me to Mercutia Road on a Friday and left me, maybe for good. She knocked on the door and I dropped back to the fifth step so I could breathe. Snow was coming down like feathers and I thought of Trim and Grace and our three-way knot. But mostly I thought of Miko and the last hug he'd given me that morning. In my mind I was hugging him back again and again and thinking maybe it wasn't the end after all, maybe he'd break the rules and send me a letter sometime, or I'd walk down the street one day and there he'd be, smiling.

'Holly,' he'd said. 'You'll be fine. I know.'

'Yeah, Miko. Fine.'

'Just remember. The mattress trick. And cracking each day open—'

'Yeah, yeah, like a nut.'

'That's it, Holly. You're a class act.'

But it wasn't like he'd given me his personal mobile number or anything.

I shivered on those steps that morning in the snow in Tooting Bec.

'You all right, Holly?' said Rachel.

'Yeah. Fine. 'S cold.'

'I know.' She touched my arm, then stamped her feet on the top step.

The door opened. Fiona was there, nodding like one of those daft dogs they have in the back of cars. 'Come on in. It's perishing.'

I walked over the doormat and I felt Fiona's hand on my shoulder. 'Holly,' she went. 'You're welcome here, you know. Truly.' The way she looked at me, she made me feel like I was her new toy. Then her voice went up a notch, to include Rachel. 'Tea's made.'

Rachel left soon after and Fiona cleared up the kitchen, humming, like it was normal to have a delinquent care-babe with a cracked-up past in her home. I stared at the wooden table and the mats on it and how the varnish looked brand new. The memory of the table back at the Home, with all the rings from hot drinks and scuffs and biro marks, made a heavy pain in my stomach. I thought of the wind-ups and Trim going ballistic and Miko juggling and Grace flicking her peas around the table instead of eating them. *Why did I agree to come here?*

Five

The Wig

Days passed. New school. New place. New people. New everything. The house on Mercutia Road was grave-yard quiet. Outside, snow came and went, day in and day out.

Fiona kept starting conversations. I could never think what to say. Trouble was, she always got round to asking a question, so I had to say *something*. It was like she was trying to nose me out. I wasn't a buried bone, for God's sake. I tried not to be in the same room with her.

My favourite place was the stairs. I'd counted sixty-three, including the ones outside. I'd sit on the second landing, where the stairs bent round on them-selves and there was a tiny window. I'd watch the snow fall and the sky go empty. Some days Rosabel'd sit in my lap, others she'd lie low on my bed.

When Fiona wasn't looking, I'd go rooting around. I'd be in the drawers and cupboards, check-ing the place over, sniffing for anything that might start a new thought. But I only found boring stuff.

Sheets, towels, sachets of lavender. Everything just so.

Then, after a week in the new house, I found the wig.

It was in the bottom drawer of a chest at the very top of the sixty-three stairs in a plastic bag so skinny I nearly didn't bother looking inside. But I dipped my hand in for a mystery feel and touched thin strands, all scrunched and soft. So I had to look in. It was pretend hair, some almost grey, some gold, but overall blonde, with muted highlights. I took it out and fingered its layers and fringes. Inside, a net with a brown tape for keeping it on. When you held it over your fist, the white of your own skin shone through where the parting was, like scalp.

A wig, ash-blonde, drop-dead gorgeous.

'Holly!' came Fiona's voice from downstairs. 'Holly – lunch!'

I stuffed the wig back and shut the drawer. I promised myself when Fiona left the house to go shopping that afternoon, I'd try it on.

Downstairs, Fiona was looking like the last whale had been harpooned. It was Saturday and Ray'd gone to work, which he shouldn't have. I sat down at the kitchen table and picked at my food, but I wasn't hungry. That wig had really got to me. I tapped my toes on the floor. Then Fiona and I had our first row, a real wang-dammer.

When I got wound up in the Home and it got to be too much, it was like Miko said, a nail bomb went off. Anything near me went on a real hard flying lesson. Cushions. Chairs. Trainers. And Miko would come and clamp me down and my arms would be windmills and I'd swear and kick and it felt good. Then he'd say, 'Do the mattress trick, Holly.' I'd run from the room, go upstairs, yank my mattress off the bed, and kick it as hard as I could. He said to do it every morning and evening, even when I wasn't angry. I'd hammer the springs with my trainer soles and then collapse, sweat pouring. And the others couldn't wind me up so easily.

But that lunch with Fiona, I forgot the mattress trick. And anyway, my bed on Mercutia Road had a mattress too thick for lifting unless you were King Kong. I just wanted Fiona to hurry up and go out, so I could try the wig on.

'Sure you don't want to come shopping?' she was going. 'You could choose your pizzas.'

'Nah. Rather stay here. Honest.'

'Sure?'

'Yeah. It's wet.'

'There are such things as umbrellas, you know. You haven't been out in two days.'

I pushed a tomato slice across the plate. 'It's cold.'

'You don't like the cold?'

'Nah.'

'D'you prefer the summer?'

See what I mean about the questions? 'Yeah. S'pose.'

Fiona reached over to the bread board for another slice. 'Call me odd, but I love the winter. January's my favourite month.'

Would she *never* go?

'Wish you'd try my bread, Holly, love.'

Now I can't stand it when people call you 'love' when they hardly know you. For me that's a wind-up to end all wind-ups.

'It's home made,' she said. 'Honest-to-God flour. Wholemeal.'

I put a finger down my mouth. 'Ick.'

'Don't do that, Holly, please.'

I did it again.

'Don't! I make all this food, but you just eat rubbish, pure rubbish, instead. It's a wonder your insides haven't seized up with all that refined artificial stuff you put down yourself.'

'With all that refeened arty-farty stuff you put down *your*self,' I said and pretended to throw up over the loaf.

Fiona snatched it away, leaving the bread knife behind, and went over to the kitchen worktop. She rattled at the bread bin.

'Refeened, arty-farty,' I said, wagging a finger at where the loaf had been.

'Come on, Holly. Leave off. I've a good mind to call Rachel. Perhaps we need a talk.'

The nail bomb burst. I picked up the bread knife and hurled it at the kitchen window. It missed and clattered into the sink. So I stood up, grabbed my chair and slammed the far leg into a kitchen cupboard.

'Fucking bread, fucking kitchen,' I screamed. 'Go on, say it. You want me gone, Ray wants me gone, you hate the sight of me. And I hate your fucking fancy bread and I hate you too. I'm not your child. I don't want to be your child. I'm Mammy's child, not yours.'

Fiona came over and put her hands on my shoulders. 'Holly! Calm down.'

I hated her touching me with her mad hot fingers. I shoved her out the way and ran from the room.

I went upstairs. I slammed my bedroom door and locked it. She came and knocked a few minutes later.

'Holly?'

'Go away, Mrs Empty-Ovary.'

Silence.

Then Fiona again. 'What was that you just called me?'

'Nothing.'

'No. It wasn't nothing, Holly. What did you say?'

I didn't answer.

She went away again. Ten minutes later she was back.

'I'm going out to the shops,' she called through the door. Her voice was wavy like it had tears in it. 'When I get back I hope you'll be ready to apologize.'

There was silence. Then I heard her go away.

Soon as I heard that front door slam downstairs, I unlocked my door and went straight up to the top of the house to get the wig.

Six

Call Me Solace

I reached the top landing, took the wig out of the drawer and rushed back to my room. All the time it felt like someone was watching me. A ghost, a bad ghost, out to get me.

I locked my door behind me to try to shut it out, but it followed me right under the crack.

I sat at the mirror with my head down and breathed out. Then I pulled on the wig.

I raised my head and stared in the glass. The room seemed to get darker. Outside, the rain had turned to snow. The hair of the wig and my own baby-fine brown hair were muddled round the edges. It was half Holly Hogan and half a crazy stranger. *Stay cool, girl,* I told myself. *Tidy up.*

My heart thumping, I tucked in the stray dark bits. Then I brushed down the magic ash-blonde strands, combing them forward, then back, straightening the parting.

When I'd finished, I put down the brush and took another breath. I switched on the bedside lamp, so that the shadows fell back to the room's edges. Then I looked back in the glass.

And there she was.

The new girl on the block.

She was three years older than Holly Hogan, dead smart, a real cool glamour girl.

Grace told me all about glamour girls. They have slim-slam hips, she said, and they blow smoke rings at all the mogits. They have the whole world at their feet.

In this girl's eyes was a bit of Mam. She was halfway between Holly and Mrs Bridget Hogan. But she was soaring above us both on the way to a different life. She was the kind of girl you can only watch, you can never be.

Her eyes blinked. Her mouth opened. I picked up the hairbrush again. I reached for the shell box and put on Mam's old amber ring. It was big for my ring finger, so I put it on the next one up. Mam's voice was in my head, talking to me, the way she used to when I was brushing her hair, back in the sky house. I was brushing and staring through the mirror to the other side, where the clouds bumped up against the window, way above the ground. Mam smiled back in her halter-neck dress, the one that showed off her cream shoulders and hugged her above the knees. Her hair was shiny curls but her eyebrows were dark, like frowns. She had her see-through drink in one hand and her lipstick in the other. She was getting ready to go out to her dancing job and I was brushing away.

'What shall we call her, Holl?' asked Mam.

We looked at the new girl on the block.

'Dunno. Something fancy.'

We thought.

Then Mammy had it. 'D'you remember the horse? The horse you chose that time? That Denny put the money on?'

I saw a ragged row of chestnut and muscle, horses with necks stretched out like giraffes. The most beautiful horse in the world was straining at the front, different from the others, pale gold, palomino. 'Sister Solace,' I whispered. 'I remember her, Mam.'

'This girl here – same shade, right?'

'Yeah.'

'And fast?'

'A winner.'

'So we'll call her Solace, Holl. After the horse.'

'Solace?' The locks kissed my cheeks. 'Yeah. After the horse, Mam. 'S perfect. That's who I am. I'm a girl called Solace. And I'm on the move. And nobody tells me what to do.'

'That's right, Holl. You've got the picture.' She put a hand on mine. 'Don't stop brushing, Holl, for love nor money.'

I kept brushing for love and for money. 'Solace,' I said with every stroke. 'Call me Solace.' And I was Solace, Solace of the road, walking into a night sky, thumb out and fag in hand. I was off to Ireland, where Mammy was and where the grass was green. I wasn't sure what town she was in, but I'd find her. I would. I'd cross the Irish Sea and walk up the Irish hills in the fine, soft rain, drinking in the fresh air by the pint, just like Mammy promised. Nobody was going to stop me and I was going, going—

Downstairs a door slammed.

The sky house vanished. Ireland vanished. It was Tooting Snooting again with the snow floating down outside and the silence inside.

Fiona, back from the shops already. I smiled a Solace smile, a halo-light slanting round my smooth crown. I looked good, but I was a real mad, bad girl.

'Holly,' Fiona called from the hall below. 'Come and see what I got.'

I took off the wig and hid it under my pillow with Rosabel sitting on top. 'Back soon,' I promised.

I unlocked the door and went downstairs, my hand skimming the banister.

I went and lounged against the kitchen door. 'Hi, Fiona.'

She'd got ham and pineapple pizza.

'My fave. Thanks.' I was so hungry I could have eaten it there and then.

'Let's forget about earlier, shall we, Holly?'

Fiona looked straight at me. I couldn't look away. 'Yeah, Fiona,' I said. 'OK.'

'As long as you don't call me that name again.'

I stood at the kitchen door, fingering the zip on my top.

'You won't, will you, Holly? Please?'

'No, Fiona.' Then I said something Miko used to say. 'I hear you.'

Fiona smiled. 'Thanks. You see, it's a sore spot that I can't have children.' She reached into the shopping and took out a bag of clementines and offered me one. 'A few years back I had cancer.'

I took a clementine, forgetting how I hated peeling them. 'Cancer?'

'No worries now. The doctors say I'm all clear. But I had to have chemotherapy. Do you know what that is?'

I tossed the clementine from one hand to the other like it was a ball. 'Uh-uh.'

'It's when they give you these drugs and your hair falls out and you feel sick. Sometimes afterwards it means you can't have children.'

I stared at the dimples on the orange skin. 'Ick,' I managed.

'A small price to pay to be alive but it wasn't what Ray or I wanted. So don't call me that name again, Holly. Please.'

'OK,' I said.

Fiona nodded and started unpacking the rest of the shopping. I watched her. Then I put the clementine down and picked a bag up and took out the tins of tomatoes. I put them in the cupboard where I thought they went.

'That time . . .' Fiona went on, opening the freezer door. She stuffed in some frozen fish. 'The longest eighteen weeks of my life. I wore this wig to cover up the hair-loss.'

'A wig?'

'Yes, ash-blonde. I hated it. It made my cheeks look red, but not healthy red, more blotchy. I tried scarves but then you might as well tattoo CANCER VICTIM

33

on your forehead. The whole thing was like a nightmare happening to someone else, Holly. Know the feeling?'

'Telling me,' I said.

'At the time I put on a brave face. Then, after it was over, I was a mess. Now, when I look back, I get the creeps. I thought my hair would never grow back, but it did. Only differently.' She picked up a strand of her wavy hair, smiling at me from across the kitchen. 'It was straight before. Now look at it. What was the worst time in your life?'

I was halfway up to the cupboard with a bag of brown rice. I froze, staring at the strand of Fiona's light-brown hair, not unlike my own. *The secure unit. The night out with Grace and Trim when the police collared me. Being stuck on that train with the raving drunks that time I ran away.* The memories crashed around in my head. *That other time, with Mam and Denny in the sky house . . .*

I couldn't speak. Fiona smoothed her hair back behind her ear. I put the rice on the worktop and walked past her fast.

Didn't say anything, as if she hadn't asked anything.

'Holly?' Fiona called after me. Then something about how I'd forgotten my clementine. But I was already halfway up the stairs.

I thought I'd just go take another look at Solace, up there under my pillow.

Seven

More Snooting Heck

The winter months passed and I was frozen solid while everyone else rushed by. I knew time moved only because of the tick-tock-no-luck carriage clock on the Aldridges' mantelpiece, a fancy gold affair that chimed the hours and puttered on like life was muffled up in cotton wool.

Fiona kept on at her job, three days a week. She taught reading to backward kids and was always going on about books and why didn't I have any. She had that in common with Miko. Sometimes Miko would wring his hands and say, 'Go read a book or something, lads,' and it was like asking us to fly to Mars. To Fiona I said that I had my mags and they were better than books because books were boring. Fiona had them creeping up every wall, shelves of them. I'd never seen so many. They freaked me out because they reminded me of school.

School was the pits. The teachers were pit-miseries, every last one. Mrs Atkins, the English teacher, was the worst. I'd arrived just as the class was starting *Jane Eyre* and finishing up the war poets – this stuff by long-gone soldiers who thought war was a waste of space. They banged on about wires and gas attacks and mates who copped it. 'Holly,' Mrs Atkins said one class. 'Are you listening?'

'Yeah, miss.' English class had an odd number in it and the desks were arranged in pairs, so Little Miss New Girl was marooned off to the side.

'What did I just say?'

'How the war poets are great 'n' all.'

'But what *precisely* did I say, Holly?'

I screwed up my face. 'Oh, yeah. How the great thing about the war poets is they're dead, miss.'

The class laughed. Mrs Atkins looked like I'd stabbed her in the eye.

'Very funny. Hilarious. Turn to our new book, *Jane Eyre*, Holly. The author of that is dead too, you'll no doubt be thrilled to hear. Please read from the beginning.'

I picked up this paperback with a woman in an old-fashioned long dress walking under trees, thinking, *Jeez, not another pile of old dead crap*. There was this long introduction and the class tittered while I fumbled through the pages to find the start. '*There weren't no possibility taking a walk that day,*' I read out in my most bored, Cockney accent. That killed the class. So I kept droning on about the rain and the window seat and the bird book, and it was the biggest pile of jaw-dropping junk you ever heard, and when I got to the bit where the bad cousin John throws a book at her I was glad. She was such a whiner, that Jane. Then Mrs Atkins said to stop because her ears were about to fall off and the whole class laughed and I wanted to throw the bloody book at Mrs Atkins but the bell went, so I didn't.

Later that morning, the class toughie, a townie called Karuna, had a go at me. She stood on a chair and read from the book the wrong way up and did my Cockney accent and then jumped to the ground saying her ears were falling off and the whole class laughed again. She grabbed my dinner money cheque that I happened to be holding and read it out loud. I tried to snatch it back, but too late. She'd found out I wasn't normal. It had my name, Hogan, written on one side, and Fiona's – Aldridge – signed on the other. She shouted out to the whole class that I was a bastard. I got her by the neck and yanked her thick fair hair and she screamed and Mr Preston came in and I nearly got excluded. He sent me to the head and the head said another time it would be curtains. When I got back to class, Mr Preston made me say sorry to Karuna in front of everyone.

'Sorry, Karuna,' I went. I made my voice go all velvety syrup: *Sooorrry, Karrrooona.* We glared at each other and it was *Takes one to know one.* I couldn't help it: I smiled and she grinned back. We were two cats on a case. At break time she gave me a fag and we swapped mobile numbers. Then the next day she ignored me, on account of her mate Luke coming back from Tenerife. Least that's what he made out, but he didn't have a tan. So I was back to being Little Miss

New Girl. An unending Holy Bloody Day of Obligation, as Mam used to say.

Evenings, I got home and lay down on the sofa with the TV remote and my pizza. I asked Fiona if I could have a TV for my room and she said no.

'Everyone at school's got a TV in their room,' I said.

'We're not everyone.'

Empty-Ovary, I thought. 'But—'

'OK, OK, I'll think about it.' Maybe she phoned Rachel or something, but the next day she said I could have a small one. I had to pay towards it from my pocket money every week and turn it off by eleven and I agreed.

I'd never had a TV in my room before. Nor such a snappy mobile. It was only pay as you go, but it folded small and light. Fiona got it for me because my last one was broken. I sent a text to Trim and Grace straight off, so they'd know my new number. HRU. GR8 HERE. LUV H.

Only it wasn't GR8 here.

You'd think I'd have died and gone to heaven with the room, the mobile, the TV. What more could a care-babe want? But it was wrong somehow. I was an odd-ball in that house, a crackhead in a yoga class.

Take the fags for instance.

I didn't tell Fiona and Ray I smoked. They were too squeaky-clean. So I'd puff a fag out my bedroom window.

One Saturday, Ray found one of my butts.

'Hey, Holly,' he called. He was in the back garden

38

and my window was ajar. I stuck my nose out. There was a flutter in the air like something new in the breeze. He smiled up at me. It was the kind of smile people put on when they didn't mean to catch your eye.

'What?'

He held up a butt, camel-coloured, and twizzelled it round like a cocktail umbrella. 'This yours?' he said.

'Nah. Nothing to do with me.'

'Maybe the wind dropped it there?'

'Yeah, Ray,' I said. 'That must have been it. The wind. A great big puff.'

He shook his head like the world was a sad case and tossed it in the bin with the garden rubbish. 'I used to smoke, you know,' he said, picking up the hedge clippers.

'That so?'

'Yeah. But I realized it's a mug's game. So I cut it out.' He started at the hedge.

Clip-clop went Ray's shears all afternoon. I shut the window and drew the curtains to be more private. I could have murdered a fag. But so much of my pocket money was going on the TV, I didn't have a penny to get any. So I lit a pretend fag and played at being the great glamour girl herself, Solace. I painted my nails hot red and jiggled in front of the mirror with the wig on plus my bikini top and shortest skirt. My mam used to dance in all the top clubs in Mayfair and she made a packet. She had a slinky body-suit with spangles and ostrich feathers, the works. And for sure, I thought, she's up there now in Ireland in some posh joint, breaking hearts, and that's where I'm headed too, back to Ireland, where Mam and I started, and I'm joining her up on that stage and we'll be a double act.

Ask me if I remember Ireland and it's like a painting that's still wet, running in the rain. I was five when we left on the boat for England. All I remember is flashes. A fly buzzing round a yellow lampshade, laughter coming from another room, a tall spire, and down the street a bridge where I dropped sticks into a black river.

And that's where Mam lived now. She was there and I was here and it was a mistake. She'd had to leave England in a hurry and meant to send for me, but before she could, the social services came and took me away, and now she didn't know where to find me. My big plan was to go back under my own steam and find her myself. I'd find her on a billboard in her slinky dance gear, back in Cork, the town we came from first. Dancing with the wig on, making me older, it was like getting a step closer. *I'm coming, Mam.* Jiggle, jiggle, slim-slam. *Wherever you are, I'll find you. Clip-clop* went Ray's shears below. Then the light changed and the wig seemed to change colour too. A freak hail shower rattled the windowpane behind the curtain.

I smiled. The hail was a sign.

Imagine the wind on your face, girl, I thought to myself. Imagine the looks from the men. Imagine the cars and the wheels fizzing on the roads and the fields, the green hills and the small towns passing. Imagine

Ireland and the daft dogs and shiny pavements and people dancing the night away in the bars, going cracked with the music and the jokes.

Imagine freedom, Holly. Imagine.

Eight

Coasters

Rachel called over soon after to check out the placement. We all sat in the living room on two fat sofas
under this fancy light creation that hung over the
coffee table. It had eight twisted arms with tiny naked
lights at the end, like some freaky octopus. The carriage
clock tick-tocked. Fiona, Ray and Rachel drank
tea, with their cups all neat on these raffia mats that
Fiona called coasters. I had Coke, ditto. Fiona chatted
brightly as if we were one happy house of coves.
She didn't say anything about the time I called her
that name.

'Are *you* happy, Holly?' Rachel said.

'Yeah. Fine,' I said.

'Do you miss the Home?' she said.

'Nah.'

'Miko's gone now. Did you know?'

I shouldn't have been surprised but I was. 'Gone?'

'He's got this new job with young offenders. He's
gone north over the river, Finchley way.'

I thought of Miko, crossing the river, and *pfuff!*

going, gone, because of the rules saying it was the end of all contact. All the yarns about his mad Irish family in County Mayo, 'so help me God', and a million and one first cousins, and the time he hitched from one end of France to another, gone. His missing front tooth and shaved head and the way he could dribble a football round Trim, gone. He'd be juggling and crooning away to a load of dimwit delinquents who'd smash in his face the first chance they got.

'Do you want me to give him a message?' Rachel said.

'A message?'

'Like "Good luck in your new job" or something? You were friends, you and Miko, weren't you?'

'S'pose.'

'So you must have a message for him?'

I shrugged. Fiona asked if I wanted another Coke. I said yes. She went out to the kitchen to get it. Silence. Ray asked Rachel if she was from around here. I sucked in a cheek and drew a spiral with the tip of my trainer on the swanky cream rug. Templeton House was shrinking smaller with every circle. Grace, Trim and Miko were three fuzzy dots and the years there a dream that had never been. I saw Miko going north, crossing the bridge over the river with Big Ben donging away. Then Grace, practising her dainty walking so she could be a supermodel. And Trim, with his plans to become a millionaire from the chain of casinos he was going to open. Grace and Trim, scheming together and not ever texting me. And Miko, not even writing a card to say goodbye. Fiona came back with my drink. I got up and cruised past her, saying nothing.

In my room, I put Solace on. I brushed her down and Mam was in the mirror again, telling me to brush away for all Ireland, and I swear I could hear the lift in the sky house coming to take her away to her night job, droning as it rose flight by flight.

'Holly?'

It was Fiona, knocking on my door.

'Rachel's gone,' she called. 'She said to say goodbye. Are you OK?'

'Yeah.'

'You're very quiet.'

'Yeah.'

'Can I come in?'

I stashed the wig away under my pillow and lay on the bed with Rosabel scrunched to my belly. 'S'pose.'

Her face came round the door, pale and smiling. 'You're very snug.'

'Yeah. Ta.'

'Are you all right, Holly? Are you *really* all right?'

' 'M fine.'

'Only you look like you've been crying.'

I fiddled with Rosabel's ears.

'Ray and I were wondering. Do you want to pop over to Templeton House? Ray said he'd drive you. Next weekend, maybe?'

I shrugged, like it was all in a day. Then I thought, seeing Grace and Trim again, it'd be like old times. I thought about what Grace would say about my new zip-up skater top. She'd say I needed to drop the zip

44

three inches. And Trim would practise his tae kwon do on me.

'OK. If you like, Fiona.'

She grinned. 'Great, Holl. I'll tell Ray.' She shut the door behind her.

Holl?

Only *Mammy* called me that.

I threw Rosabel hard against the door panel where Fiona's face had been.

But the next weekend she remembered the promise and Ray drove me to Templeton House.

It was the same, only different. Same smell, different people. It felt empty without Miko. Grace fluttered her eyelashes and stroked her supermodel neck and talked about her new mate, Ash. It was Ash this, Ash that. Her voice was vague and she'd laugh for no reason and I figured she'd done some skunk, which she'd got into just before I left.

'Where's Trim?' I asked.

'Trim? He's back in the secure unit. Where the hell else? Serves him.'

'Why? What'd he do now?'

'Slashing car tyres or something. Whatever. Who cares? Trim and I are history,' she droned, and laughed some more.

I wanted to check out my old room, to see if the gold lamé curtains were still there, but it was Ash's now. In the end, it was better to say my foster dad was outside waiting and I couldn't stop.

'So long, Grace,' I said.

She stared at her fingernails as if she'd just had a

manicure. The cuticles were torn and red. She'd been picking at them with her nail scissors. She stroked her neck some more.

'See you around, Grace,' I said. I went up close on account of her eyes were filling like she was about to cry. I wanted to touch her beauty braids but didn't dare. 'Grace?'

'You're a witch, Holly.' She said it like a spit.

'A witch. Me?'

'Yeah, you. You and your fancy new foster home. Fucking cow-witch. That's what Trim said, before they took him away.'

'I'm not.'

'Yeah, you are.

I shrugged. 'The foster place. 'S not that great, really, Grace.'

'No?'

'No.'

'Why not?'

'Dunno. They fuss.'

'Fuss?'

'Yeah. They nag.'

'Nag?'

'All bleeding day. Nag, nag.'

'How nag?'

'Like I can't put things down on the table without a mat.'

Grace's nose wrinkled. 'A mat?'

'Yeah, you know. To stop the stains. Only they call them coasters.'

'Coasters?'

'Yeah. It's posh talk for a mat.'

'Coasters.' She said *cooosters*, all lah-di-dah, and I laughed. 'Pull down that zip, Holly. You look like a bloody nun with it up round your neck like that.'

I pulled the zip down to my bra-line.

'Mr and Mrs Coooster,' she crooned, and we fell about laughing.

'So it's not as good there as here?' Grace's hands fluttered, gesturing round the room.

'Nah. No way.'

'So why don't you come back?'

I made like I was blowing out a cloud of smoke. 'Ash is in my room now. Remember?'

'Oh, yeah. Ash. So?'

'So. I wouldn't want to share with no Ash.'

'Ash is only temporary.'

I fiddled with my zip, shuffled my feet. 'When she's gone, maybe I'll be back then.'

'Huh. You're a liar.' She knew and I knew. Templeton House was a one-way turnstile. 'You're not coming back, Holly. I can tell. You're a cow-witch.' The next second she was off the sofa and drifting out the door before I could answer. Her brown shoulders were shaking up and down. I couldn't tell if she was laughing or crying.

'Grace,' I yelled. 'Don't go.'

The door swung to behind her. She was going clean out of my life like she'd never been.

'Grace?' I cried. 'Please. Come back.'

No reply.

Cow-witch yourself, I thought. I kicked the chair

where she'd been sitting. I looked around the old familiar room and thought of the fights over what to watch and Trim raving on about *Titanic*. The TV was on with the sound turned down and the weather woman wearing her worst mogit jacket was pointing at the map of England with that cheesy grin weather people always have, especially if rain's coming. I found the remote and turned it off. Then I kicked the remote under the sofa so nobody'd find it.

That'll teach them, I thought.

If Ray and Fiona send me back here, I thought, I'll kill myself.

I left that room for the last time and I walked out the front door on my own with nobody to say goodbye to, just Ray waiting outside. I walked down the drive, looking at the cracked path with weeds in it, and I wanted to burn the place to the ground.

I got into Ray's car and on the way back I stared out the side window. I didn't want Ray to see my leaky eyes. He put a tape on of some weirdo band I'd never heard of and hummed along. The music was soft and dreamy with this woman's voice going on about how this guy flies a plane and makes the jet trail write her name in the sky.

'Yeah, right,' I muttered. 'Like anyone would ever do that.'

Ray smiled. 'Ah, but can't you just picture it?' He waved a hand at the sky. '*Holly Hogan*, up there in letters so big it's all anyone can see. Your name's made out of cloud, Holly.'

I kept looking out the window. I didn't say anything.

'So,' he asked as the song ended. 'How did you find it?'

I didn't know if he meant the song or the Home. I started sobbing loud and couldn't stop. It was the thought of my name shining in the sky, like in the song, and Miko, looking up from north London and maybe seeing it and remembering me. I couldn't hide it. My face was mashed. Ray stopped the car. He found a hanky and passed it over but didn't say anything. I felt him waiting.

'Huh, Holly,' he grunted after a bit. 'That bad?'

That nearly set me off again, but he started up the car and drove on and I swallowed it down so it sat like a heavy dinner in my belly. He said nothing more. I wanted to die with shame. I cursed Grace and Trim and Miko and the Home and the social services. Then I cursed the Aldridges and Rachel. Then I cursed myself and the song and the coasters and everything I could see from the car, and when it started hammering with rain I was glad.

Nine

Solace of the Road

That night I smuggled Ray's road map of Britain up to my room. *It's time to get serious, girl,* I thought. I looked up the roads from London, north, south, east and west. I found one, a long rambling snake, that went west. Some roads joined up with others and ran out. This one, the A40, didn't. Oxford. Cheltenham. My fingers traced out the towns. It went right through Wales. Abergavenny. Llandovery. Llandeilo. Carmarthen. I said the names even though I didn't know how they were pronounced. Lan-day-low. Lando-very. The road hit the sea at a place called Fishguard. Then a dotted line kept on going over the sea like a road, only it was the path the ferries took. On the coast of Ireland, at the edge of the page, the dotted line bumped into Rosslare.

I thought myself onto a hill above Fishguard with sheep baaing. Below were fields, wavy squares of tall crops. Beyond that was a great wall of blue. The sea, where white sails headed west to Ireland.

I put the wig on and I thought myself into Solace

of the A40, and the A was for Adventure and the wig was glittering in the evening light. I was Solace the Unstoppable, the smooth-walking, sharp-talking glamour girl, and I was walking into a red sky, ready to hitch a ride. I was crossing the sea and landing in Ireland. Then I was walking up a hill to meet my mam, breathing in the morning air by the pint. That is how I thought myself into the sweet, soft day on the other side of the sea where the grass is green. That night and every night for weeks to come, I traced the road.

Ten

The Iron

It was summer before I turned my dream real, a hot day in June, the day before my birthday. I opened my window over the purple-grey roofs and breathed. The air shone clean and white over the common.

It was the kind of day that pulls you out to play.

Downstairs, Ray was late for work and Fiona was ironing him a shirt. Ray hopped around the kitchen chivvying her and I sat with a bowl of Krispies and my music on. Fiona and Ray didn't argue much because first, Ray was hardly there, and second, when he was he never said much. Fiona moaned that arguing with him was like arguing with a hat stand. But that morning they did argue, big time. I saw him waving his hands in the air like he was drowning. He snatched at the shirt before it was ironed enough. Curious, I pulled out my earphones.

'It's not finished,' Fiona snapped.

'It's fine, Fee. I'm late.'

'The sleeves are still creased.'

'I'll wear the jacket. They won't see.' He grabbed the shirt off the ironing board.

'But it's boiling out there. Too hot for a jacket.'

'It's air-conditioned at work.'

'You never normally bother with a jacket.'

'I've got an important meeting.'

'A meeting?'

'Well, Fee. Kind of. Actually, an interview.'

'Interview? What interview?'

Ray shrugged, putting on the crumpled shirt. 'Just a chat, nothing—'

'*What* interview?'

'Just some job.'

'What job? Where?'

'Our firm, still. Up in the northern office, only—'

'*Northern* office?' Fiona squeaked.

I thought of Miko crossing the river, going north. Maybe Ray was heading after him.

'You didn't tell me,' Fiona was shouting. 'You didn't ask me.'

'It's only—'

Fiona slammed the iron down and stalked out. Only she didn't put the iron down properly and it fell off the board and crashed to the floor and nearly landed on Ray's foot. A drawer in my brain slid open. I froze. Ray jumped, then saw me watching and smiled, a funny smile like he and me were on one side and the iron and Fiona were on the other. I slammed the drawer shut. I put the earphones back in and turned up the volume, loud. I pushed away the

Krispies and ran upstairs, my heart pounding to the beat of Storm Alert.

The iron was a sign.

Fiona was going downstairs as I was going up.

'What's the rush?' she wailed. 'Why's everyone in a rush today?'

I shrugged. In my room, I pulled on my school clothes and crept down again and headed for the door, my head racing ahead of itself with plans.

'Bye, Fiona,' I yelled like everything was normal. Maybe it was too loud on account of my music. Fiona appeared in the hall, mouthing something.

'What, Fiona?' I bawled. I pulled out the earphones.

'I *thought* you couldn't hear me with those things in. It's like talking to a wall.' She came towards me. 'Look, Holl . . .'

The nailbomb nearly blew.

'It's just to say I'll be late today,' Fiona said. 'You've got your key?'

'Yeah.'

'There's something I've got to do – a certain something for a certain somebody. Let yourself in and have a sandwich. I'll be home by six or so.'

I nodded. She looked into my eyes and gave this strange smile. 'Bye, Fiona,' I said and headed out the door.

To get to school I had to cross the common and catch a bus. But that morning I peeled off towards the pond. I sat down on a broken bench and waited. My hands were shaking at the thought of the hot iron landing on the floor by Ray's foot and I could hear it spitting like they do when you put water on the flat side. There was a sizzling in my brain. I had to concentrate to breathe, as if a plastic bag was over my head. It was only the air and the green grass that saved me from smothering. The sun shone hard and bright. I shut my eyes because the sky house was coming back with the voices of Denny and Mammy, bicker-bicker, their voices going up and up like the lifts did. I concentrated on the ducks squawking, biting each other. The whole world was fighting, with me squashed up in the middle.

This Aldridge crap's killing me, I thought. They're not my kind. I've gotta get out. Now.

I pictured Miko, with his shaved head and grin, walking up a dusty highway with his thumb sticking out, going from one end of France to the other. And I pictured the A40 snaking its way across England, heading like a river to the sea.

A for Adventure, I thought.

And I smiled. I walked back over the grass the way I'd come, fingering the key to Mercutia Road in my pocket.

I'd done with school and the pit-miseries. I'd done with Tooting Snooting. I'd done with Rachel and the reviews and rules and reports. I'd done with everything. From now on it was me and the wig, and together we made a girl called Solace. And Solace was on her way. Today.

Last time I'd done a runner I'd gone out the door with nothing. I wasn't making that mistake again.

I let myself back into the house with my key. Fiona had left for her part-time job and Ray had gone to his job with plans and buildings and other mogit stuff up town. And his interview. I closed the front door behind me. The hallway had a sad, waiting-room feel. The whole house was quiet. I couldn't wait to be gone but I had to fetch my things, not to mention the wig. I was running away serious this time. I had a plan.

I went upstairs and got out my best lizard-skin bag. I put in:

My toothbrush.
iPod and earphones.
Lipstick and mirror.
Hairbrush.
Mobile phone.
Furry pink purse.

Then I went to the shell box on the mantelpiece and got out Mammy's amber ring. It was like a good-luck charm, golden brown and shaped like an old-fashioned tombstone. In the middle was a black speck, like an insect. Miko'd told me it was a fossil from a world long gone, trapped there for all time. *They'd chop your finger off for a ring like that, Holl,* Mam's voice echoed in my head. I smiled and put it safe in the secret zip-up pocket of the lizard-skin bag.

Then I picked up Rosabel from my pillow. I stroked her worn-out ears. '*Grrr-rap!*' I said.

It was a wrench, but she was too big to fit in the lizard. And with the wig on I was seventeen, not

56

fourteen, too old to be carrying round a toy dog. I put her back on the bed, and her black plastic snout went down between her front paws.

I changed into my best skater stuff, including the new top and my trainers.

Then I went round the house looking for money. I already had six quid in my own purse. I found a tenner in one of Ray's jackets plus loads of loose change in his trouser pockets. He'd never miss it. I got up to twenty-four quid. Then I got the road map out. I nearly tore out the pages that showed the A40. Then a light bulb came on in my head. *Ding. Dumbo. They'll know where you're going if you leave it looking like that.* So I took the whole thing, thinking I could chuck the parts I didn't need later.

In the kitchen I saw the ironing board still up and the iron on it. A blanket went over my brain. There was an off-white light, stale and drab, as if a bulb was about to blow. 'Time to go, Mr and Mrs Empty-Ovary,' I said out loud. I went back to the living room, only there was no living going on there, just me and the carriage clock and the coasters. That's the last time I'm going to be told off about putting my mug straight on the table, like coffee rings are a sin, I thought.

Was I really going to go?

Yep.

Last time I ran away, I ended up in the secure unit.

This time, I'm off to a whole new life in a whole new country.

Then I put on the wig. There was a mirror over the carriage clock, gold round the edges. I put my head down and my own hair disappeared into the rim. I pulled the tabs down in front of my ears and scrunched them into my temples. I looked up. I was a Shetland pony. The fringe was too low. So I pulled it back and brushed it out and put my doll-pink lipstick on. Enter a glamour girl, a girl on the move. Enter Solace.

I pouted. I blew myself a kiss. Solace was a case. She didn't care what other people thought. She had a lorry-load of friends littered over half Ireland. She had a place to go. Cool as a breeze I wrote a note:

Dear Fiona and Ray,
I've gone to Tenereef to work in a club with my mate Drew who sent me tickets and all so don't bother coming after me, see you and ta for everything,
Holly

I looked at the note and added an X by the 'Holly'. Then I put my key tidy on the note. Then I left the house. The lizard was on my back, a pretend cigarette in my right hand and a crown of floating blonde upon my head. And the road ahead of me was all mine.

Eleven

The Tube

I went down the seven steps and down the street and my nose faced the way I was going. I walked with lean long limbs and my hair was smooth and neat as a trick, straight from the hairdresser's.

In Mercutia Road there was a rule that your door had to be different from the ones either side. Red. Blue. Black. Sludge grey. Blue again. Never two the same together. *If it were down to me*, I thought, *I'd paint the lot hot pink.* The sash windows stared as I went by. My hand itched to pick up a stone and hurl it but I remembered I was on the run so I just turned for the high street and made for the tube. My plan was to head as far west as I could. Every fool knows you can't hitch a ride from a city. I remembered Miko saying how in France he didn't thumb in the cities because city people think everyone else is an axe murderer so they won't stop. I had to get to the edge of London.

Hot stale air hit me as I went in the station. It reminded me of Sunday afternoons cruising with

Grace and Trim. But today it was the smell of freedom, the first leg.

Except that my Oyster card was still in my school trousers, back in Snooting Heck. Good start – now I'd have to buy a ticket.

'Child travelcard,' I told the kiosk man.

'You don't look like no child to me.'

I stared. This hadn't happened before. Then I remembered the wig. It put three years on me.

'I'm fourteen, mister,' I said. 'Honest.'

'Tell that to the marines,' he said. He winked so quick I nearly missed it. Then he tapped his machine and the travelcard flew out and I handed over the money. He scooped out the coins and motioned me on.

I took the escalator down, grinning like I'd won top prize at a beauty gala. *Tell THAT to the marines, honey.* Then a wind rushed up and I nearly lost the wig. I clamped it down with my spare hand just in time and laughed, a head-case on the loose. *Imagine freedom, girl,* the tube wind said.

I got a train right away. Balham. Clapham South. The tube hurtled north, snaking on the turns, screeching like fingernails on a blackboard. It smelled of oil and sweat. Newspapers were littered about after the rush hour. Ray would have gone this way earlier. I pictured him hanging onto the bars, his face blank and tired like it is most evenings. His newly ironed shirt would get creased again. An interview for the northern office? I realized then that it didn't mean north, as in north London, like it did for Miko going up Finchley way, because Ray *already* worked north of the river. It meant north of the country. Which meant that if he got the job he'd be moving off with Fiona, and where would that leave me? Nowhere. I bit my lip. Just as well I'd scooted. Then I heard Ray's voice like he was sitting next to me. *Your name's made out of cloud, Holly.* I shook myself and looked around. Nobody. Only a man with cuts in his jeans and tattoos on his arms, staring at me. All he needed was an axe. He had a bald head and fat cheeks and grey stubble. I stared at my feet. He did some creepy cursing and I was eyeing the emergency cord when the train pulled in at the next stop.

Clapham Common. Loads of people got on. Was I glad.

Clapham North. I'd been this way with Fiona the time we went shopping for clothes up town, and before, from Templeton House, when I rode the tubes with Trim and Grace. We'd buy drinks and fags and swagger about the platforms. Trim would act being a corporal in the army and stand to attention. He'd get a stick and bash the overhead lights like they were privates under his command. Grace would slump over the benches like a drug addict on the point of death. I'd read the small print on the adverts that said things like you could lose all your money as well as double it. In other words, ignore the big print if you've got a brain, typical mogit crap. We were bored as hell. Maybe we'd get off somewhere we'd never been before, like Dagenham Heathway. I'd picture daggers and commons and robbers and brambles but it would be roads and lorries. The daylight would make your head hurt so we'd go down and ride another tube.

Waterloo. After Waterloo you go under the river. The thought of the heavy dirty water swirling overhead made my throat tighten. What if it burst through and blew the fuse and the train exploded, and everyone drowned or fried or both? I shut my eyes. I made believe I had bubblegum. But however hard I chewed, it didn't work. I thought I'd pass out. I opened my eyes. The tattoo man was staring again. I *had* to get out. Now. I grabbed the lizard-skin bag and pushed to the door.

The tattoo guy was still cursing to himself.

I had arms and bodies and people breathing on me all around.

Embankment. The doors opened and I sprang out onto the platform. I wriggled through the crowds and rode the escalators. I got outside and breathed the air.

I was right by a flower stall.

'You all right?' the flower man said.

I jumped. 'Yeah, ta. Never better.' I pointed at some tall purple flowers with yellow centres. 'How much?'

'The irises? For you, love, two quid.'

'Another time maybe.' I waved my hand like I was a member of the royal family and walked away. I made it look like I knew where I was going, but I didn't. I felt the flower man's eyes needling my back, so I scurried down a path to the right, out of sight.

Which is how I found myself in this fancy garden I'd never even known existed. It was like going from the pits to paradise in ten metres. And isn't that London for you.

Twelve

London on a Plate

The garden was a secret. There were deckchairs with nobody sitting in them, beds of yellow, blue and red flowers and a sprinkler on the lawn and nobody out strolling, just me.

Maybe I'd dropped out of the real world. Maybe this was a dream garden. But then I found a café with white plastic seats and people scattered. Raspberry ice tea, I thought. I went in and bought it, and a million-aire bar as well. They're chocolate caramel shortcakes, the kind of thing Grace would throw up after eating on account of her supermodel dream.

Outside, I chose a table far away from any mogits. I slugged half the drink down and gobbled the bar. I sat back, eyes shut. A ball of sun floated behind my eyelids. A bird chirped. The cars zoomed along the riverbank. London churned with a million funny things. I smiled.

What next?

Maybe I could cruise back over the river on a bus to see Grace. Maybe she'd have bunked off and want to make up. Then we could check out the shops around Oxford Circus together or the action in Covent Garden. A day like this, the buskers would clean up. Maybe we could bottle for them, Grace and I. We'd collect so much money, they'd give us a fat percentage. The folks on the balcony would make paper planes from five-pound notes and fly them down at us with hoots and cat-calls. Grace the Gorgeous and Solace the Unstoppable. The buskers would adopt us as lucky mascots and soon we'd be trooping round the capitals of Europe with them and next thing I'd be wiggling my hips at the Eiffel Tower.

Then Big Ben started up and I was back in London. Dong, dong, dong. *One, two, three.*

Sometimes, when the wind was right, Mam and I could hear Big Ben strike from the sky house. Together we'd count the hour. Mam would be out on the balcony, sipping her drink. *Four, five.* Mam's dressing gown fluttered like a bride's veil, only black, not white, and under it you could see her salmon-pink slip. 'All I ever wanted,' she'd say, 'is London on a plate.' She laughed like she'd just made up the first line of a song. 'London on a bloody plate.'

Six, seven, eight. From the sky-house balcony, London was a faraway hum, a million and one other lives. Mam pointed to where the sun went down. 'That's the way to Ireland, Holl. Imagine it. The air. The greenness. The laughs. There's room to breathe there, Holl. Some day we'll go back. You and me together. Maybe we'll look up some old friends and start a whole new life. We'll have a dog. And a

64

bungalow, all our own. And a view to die for. Not like this desolation. Some day, Holl. It's a promise.'

Nine, ten, eleven. Big Ben stopped donging. Eleven o'clock. I opened my eyes. I was in the park, the sun beating down, my raspberry tea half drunk, and I was no further west than I'd been to start with.

What next? I thought.

I took out the road map and saw how I was in the middle of a giant, whole-page blob, packed with red, yellow, black and brown roads you couldn't tell apart.

Was this for real?

If they caught me they'd take me away and put me back in the secure unit. Where the walls stare and nobody answers and the rooms are bare and it smells bad. Where there's nobody to say goodnight to and you dream of falling and drawers with scary things inside open in your brain. And you hear nothing – just the voice of the guy who locked you in going, 'You ain't going nowhere, sunshine, cry all you like.'

So, I decided, this is for real and no way will they catch me. I had the wig and I had my travelcard and I was leaving.

On the map, I found the A40 and traced it back towards London. It went through Oxford, then it turned into a thick line of blue, a motorway. And that went all the way into a place called Shepherd's Bush. Shepherd's Bush, I knew from my travels with Grace and Trim, was on the tube. It wouldn't be green and lush with sheep and shepherds, it would be roads and fumes. In my head, I was already standing at the start of the motorway and sticking out my thumb.

I didn't fancy another tube ride, but it was the only way.

I tore out all the pages of the map with the A40 on it. I folded them into the lizard and got to my feet. Next I threw the rest of Ray's map in a litterbin. I felt like somebody shedding a murder weapon. I left the park fast, went down the tube and got on a Circle Line going west. I didn't think of axe murderers or flood disasters, I just spaced out to Storm Alert on full blast. At Notting Hill Gate I had to get the Central Line for Shepherd's Bush, but I needed a fag badly. The shop at the top was a mad crush so I went outside to find a newsagent's.

The sun had gone and it was spitting rain.

I put the lizard over my head to keep the wig dry. I watched the cars zoom past, and I thought of Mercutia Road and my apricot bedroom and my TV, blank, waiting to be turned on. In one more minute I'd have been down that tube riding back to Tooting Bec, end of story. But something amazing happened. A miracle. A tall, long red two-decker bus pulled up at a bus stop, with OXFORD TUBE written along the side.

'Does this bus really go to Oxford?' I asked a mogit woman at the end of the queue.

'I certainly hope so,' she said. 'That's where I'm going.' She spoke like she had grape pips up her nose.

I got in after her.

'One to Oxford,' I said to the driver. I didn't ask for 'a child ticket'. I didn't want to get caught for being unaccompanied.

He didn't even look. 'Single or return?'

66

Would my money cover it? 'Single.'

'Thirteen pounds,' he said.

Was I glad I hadn't bought any fags. I paid and he gave me a ticket. I climbed up to the top deck and found some empty seats at the back. I patted the wig dry and wiggled my slim-slam hips. *Solace, you are one mad, bad girl,* I thought. Rain bucketed outside. Ireland was one step closer. The engine started and the bus took off down a tree-lined avenue, leaving London behind us.

Thirteen

The Girl on the Bus

The bus lurched off the road and drew up near a tube station called Hillingdon. We'd come to the edge of the city. The streets had broken down to flyways and factories. It was a wilderness out there. It reminded me of how when I was little I'd stare out of the sky-house window and see the black old towers like ugly markers and I'd put my hand on the windowpane and think how I was on one side of the glass and the world on the other and what would it be like if I swapped over? The bus stopped and a moment later, a girl came up the stairs with a neat backpack and short brown curls. She walked towards me. I looked out the window hard on account of I didn't want anyone sitting by me, but the girl stopped right beside me.

'Is anyone sitting here?' she said. Another one with a snooty accent.

'Nah.'

'Do you mind?'

'Nah.'

'Thanks.'

She peeled off her bag and sat down. Rain dripped off her curls and her feet were the smallest things I ever saw, laced up in black loafers, the sort a nun would wear.

'Christ,' she said. 'Rotten day.'

'Too right.'

'You going to Oxford?'

'Yeah.'

'Me too. You studying there?'

I stroked down the wig and smiled. I don't know what came over me. I said, 'Yeah.' Me, Holly Hogan, studying at Oxford? Some joke. Mrs Atkins had despaired of me. Least I *could* read, not like Grace and Trim. They hardly knew their ABC. They used to make me read out the tube adverts to them and their texts were something else.

'I'm there too.' The girl was all smiles. 'I'm at St John's. Where are you?'

'St Peter's?' I said off the top of my head and laughed like it was just a joke.

'Oh, right,' she said. 'I don't know anyone from there. I gather the food's bad and the bar's brilliant.'

Like the place actually *existed*?

I nodded. 'Bloody bad. Bloody brilliant.' My voice had changed over from rough south Londony to grape pips to the power of ten, but this dumbo girl from hoo-haa-sint-johns didn't seem to realize.

'You a first year?' she asked.

'Yah.'

'Me too. Liking it?'

'So-so.'

'Only so-so?'

'Yah. You know. The food.'

She laughed. 'Right. The food. It's not bad at St John's.'

'It's horrible at St Peter's,' I breezed. 'D'you know what I found in my cream cracker the other day?'

'No, what?'

'A maggoty thing. Coming out of one of the holes.'

'Yikes. Sounds like a weevil. Did you report it?'

'Nah. Just chucked it.'

'Don't think I could face going back to Hall if that had happened to me,' the girl said.

Hall? Where or what was that?

She opened her bag and got out a worn-out paper-back. I made out the word 'Tacitus' on the front.

'Do you mind if I read?' she asked.

'Course not.' I'd never heard anyone ask permission to read before. But as she got into it, I almost wished I had a book too. You know what I said earlier about books being boring? But the fact is, I *do* read sometimes. When no one's looking. Not old-fashioned stories, with people getting in and out of horse-drawn carriages. That crap bores me solid. But real stories, about *now*, I can handle. Love affairs and sex. Murders. People in trouble.

The week before, at school, Mrs Atkins had organized for this writer to come and visit. She thought maybe he'd get us all wide-eyed and bushy-tailed, and made out he was some kind of celebrity, and sure enough, when he walked in I thought he was

70

typical mogit, in love with himself, skinny with shiny glasses shaped like slits in a letterbox. He's going to drone on about his ideas and his characters and his publishers, I thought, yawning. He sat down and stared at us like he didn't know how to start. Then he went, 'Does anyone here believe in modern-day miracles?'

The class tittered. Then a few hands went up. Suddenly everyone was talking about the miracles they knew about, how Grandma died of a heart attack and came back to life, how they'd met their best friend out on holiday in Majorca, or how Crystal Palace beat Man U three–nil.

And the guy nodded and said that him being here with his book *The Eleven Lives of Todd Fish* was the biggest modern-day miracle of the lot, because he'd hated school and didn't learn to read properly until he was thirteen on account of having dyslexia. Which is what Trim says he has. If you ask me it's just Trim's excuse for being thick.

'If you'd put money on me to be a writer one day,' the guy said, 'you'd have got odds of ten thousand to one and you'd be rich.'

I sat there and bit my cheek. The odds of me being a writer, I thought, are a *million* to one. But you know what? When he got us to write some sentences down about whether we believed in miracles, he liked mine so much that he read it out to the class. It made everyone laugh and he said how it was 'pithy', whatever that meant. I kept what I wrote. It goes like this:

I don't believe in miracles. My mam used to say I was a miracle but now I know about babies I know I wasn't. A miracle is more like when my mate Trim gets the ball off Miko whose the best footballer I ever saw not signed up professnall. Or like when I get pineapple on my pizza as well as ham. Its got nothing to do with god. Its luck. Luck is not the same as a miracle. Luck is what comes round the corner if you wait long enuff like the number 68 bus. Just my luck to be at this school in this class on this day in this minute having to right about miracles for this writer guy who says its a miracle he is here on account of his doing his ds and bs backwards when he was a kid. A miracle for him and not for me. Yo-ho-ho.

I remember I wrote 'right', not 'write', deliberately and loads of mistakes, but he didn't mind, nor me sending him up sky-high.

I must have chuckled out loud remembering because the girl on the bus looked up from her reading. I quickly stared out the window at the motorway hard shoulder and she went back to the book, peering at it like it was a treasure map. I glanced sideways to see what was so great about it but all I could see were words that didn't make sense.

Then the girl put the book down. 'Thule was sighted, but only from afar,' she said.

'Hey?'

'Sorry, it's this book,' she laughed. 'It's amazing. This Roman historian, Tacitus, he's writing about how Agricola – his father-in-law – sailed round Britain. And when he gets to the frozen north he sees land

72

and thinks it's Thule. But they didn't have time to reach it, or maybe it was too cold, so they sail by. And you know that Agricola must have regretted it for the rest of his life. It's like his Holy Grail, Thule.'

'Fool?' I said.

'No. Thule.' She showed me the word in the book, *Thule*.

'It's a pretty name,' I said.

'D'you have one? A place like Thule?'

'Hey?'

'A place where you always wish you could go?'

'Oh, yeah. Sure. I have a place like that. Ireland.'

'Ireland?'

'Yeah. 'S where I was born. Haven't been back in ages.'

'I hear it's gorgeous.'

'Gorgeous is right. Green, just like they say, fields and grass. What's your place?'

The girl closed her eyes and smiled. 'Egypt,' she said. 'The Valley of the Kings.'

'The mummies and all?'

'Yes. But the place I want to go to isn't the Valley of the Kings now but in nineteen twenty-two. I'm in the dig with Howard Carter and we're creeping into the tomb of Tutankhamun for the first time since it was sealed and time's stopped and we see the glint of gold . . .' Her eyes stayed shut and she moved her hand like she was finding her way through a dark passage.

'That's some Thule.'

She opened her eyes. 'You must think I'm mad.

73

That's what comes of reading dead languages. What're you reading?'

'*Jane Eyre*,' I said. Mrs Atkins would have been proud. We'd got to the bit where whiney old Jane's running away on the high moors because of Mr Rochester having a mad wife stashed away in the attic, and how stupid is that? The girl laughed. 'I meant *studying*. At Oxford.'

'Oh.' I giggled. 'French.' It was the only thing that came into my head, which is funny because I hate French even worse than English.

'French?'

I nodded.

'You mean Modern Languages?'

'Yeah.'

'Don't you have to do two?'

'Two?'

'Two languages.'

'Oh, yeah, sure thing.'

'So what's your other one?'

'Irish.'

'Irish?'

'Yep.'

'I didn't know you could study Irish at Oxford.' Her two brown eyes went wide.

'Yeah, you can. They just brought it in.'

'That's great. I mean, *really* great. Did you have any Irish to begin with?'

'Yeah. Like I said, I was born there. And my mam's Irish.'

'Does she speak it?'

'Oh, yeah.' Like she spoke Russian.

'Give me a sample – go on, I'd love to hear some.'

The coach took a turn and we were off the motor-way. The air conditioning had gone off and voices and laughter were everywhere. My ears were hot.

'In uch san, doonan micall noondee,' I said.

'Fab. What does that mean?'

'It means, "When the hell will we ever get there?"'

The girl laughed. 'Too right. I'm Chloe, by the way.'

I grinned. 'I'm Solace.'

'Solace?'

I nodded.

'Great name. But that's not Irish, is it?'

'No,' I said. 'It was my father's idea.'

'Your father?'

'Yeah. He's English. Not like my mam. He's a writer, see.'

'Wow. My father's just a CEO. I'd much rather he was a writer.'

CEO. What was that? Some sort of medal from the queen?

'So, what's his name, so I can look out for him?' Chloe asked.

'Todd Fish,' I said.

'Fish? Is that your other name then?'

God. Solace Fish? I don't think so. 'Oh no,' I breezed. 'That's just his pretend name. The name he puts on the cover.'

'You mean his *nom de plume*?'

'Not quite,' I said. ' 'S more like – his writing name.'

Maybe it was that I'd forgotten to do the posh voice, but Chloe gave me a strange look. 'Never knew there was a difference between . . .' She paused and shrugged. 'But hey. You're the French scholar.'

My cheeks were on fire. Chloe went back to her book of Holy Grails and Thules. The bus hit a roundabout and there was a sign saying OXFORD, along with a whole load of places I'd never heard of.

We dropped speed. People shuffled, stirred, yattered. We were coming into town. Oxford, here we come, I thought. The bus went down this drab street like it was anywhere place in anywhere town. But then we went round another roundabout and over a bridge and Oxford punched me in the eye. There was a big yellow tower, yellow walls and green leaves and young people walking like they owned the world, mogits before they were old. A couple going arm in arm were all in black and white and had gowns on with bat-wing sleeves.

'My boyfriend goes there,' Chloe suddenly said in my ear, jutting her head at some more yellow stone, a big pile. As the bus passed, I glimpsed a flat green lawn through the archway. In the middle a thin black statue with one arm in the air was running through the prettiest fountain I ever saw. I remembered the times Trim sprayed water on Grace and me in the back garden at Templeton House while we ran round in our bikinis. He'd throttle the neck of the hose and the water would fizz everywhere.

'Neat,' I said, smiling.

'Next year he'll be gone.'

'Gone?'

'Yeah. He's got a job with the World Bank. In Lagos.'

I never knew there was such a thing as a World Bank. I never saw a branch of it anywhere. And I didn't know where Lagos was either. 'Cool,' I said.

Chloe shrugged, closed her book and got her bag out. The bus turned and sped down some streets with concrete bollards and buildings with no windows, then squeezed into a square.

'Gloucester Green,' the driver called. He pulled into a bay and turned the engine off. Everyone was standing, grabbing, pushing to get off.

Chloe turned to me, almost smiling. 'Hey, Solace. See you around.' She shuffled out the bus.

'Bye,' I called. I watched her vanish round a corner. Then I grabbed the lizard, got off and cruised across the square. I was Solace of the road. I had a lorry-load of friends. I was so delirious I nearly got run over by a bus pulling out.

Oxford, here I come.

Fourteen

The Make-over

I coasted along a street of shops and nearly got mown down by a bicycle. There were bikes everywhere. I felt queasy just looking. It kills me how people ride them. Trim says it's easy when you get the knack but I've never tried. To me it looks like a bad circus act.

My mobile beeped. A message. DONT FORGET, HOME LATE, F. Fiona was so out of it, she didn't know to say L8.

Then I passed this shop full of wild dresses. I hadn't worn a dress in so long I couldn't remember. I stuck to jeans and sporty tops on account of being a rebel skater. I wasn't like Grace with her designer labels. Pink, flowery flounces, tights, skirts and me didn't go. But I stopped and looked in the window. I was checking the wig, mostly. But I couldn't help seeing the models in these skimpy dresses with bright colours: orange and ice-blue with chocolate-brown blobs.

The designer had taken one too many Es.

They were Solace-style, to the last stitch.

I only had four pounds left. But I could always steal. I'd done shoplifting once or twice in the small sweetshop the Asians ran near Templeton House. I'd lifted the odd chocolate bar or packet of gums, but I'd never gone for clothes. Most places have magnetic tags on everything that you can't get off without a special machine. You go through the door and an alarm goes off. You have to lift the clothes over or under the electronic beam or wrap them up in foil, according to Trim. He makes out he does it all the time. Even if the alarm starts up, he says, you scoot up the street quick, and after a block the security guards give up chasing. But I don't know if he's making it up, on account of most of what Trim says isn't true. Trim says he was born on an aeroplane and how likely is that? So I'd never lifted clothes.

On the windows of this shop someone had sprayed CLOSING DOWN. I looked over the door. The place was called Swish. I drifted inside and headed for a rack at the back. A shop girl talked on the phone like it was glued to her skull. '*Yeah, too right. I'd gone clubbing and he didn't show up on time . . . Yeah. When they let you in you can't go out again – they don't stamp you nor nothing at the Clone Zone . . . Nah. So. Shan, I was stuck . . . What? . . . Yeah. We're history . . .*'

I picked out a dress my size. It was wild – cream with mint-green and rose cloud shapes chasing each other all over, sleeveless with thin straps so your bra would show like you're a supermodel. There was no magnetic tag. I looked at the label. Eighteen pounds reduced from thirty-five.

It was off the hanger and in my lizard-skin bag, easy goes.

'. . . *He's a right scumbag and if he wants me back he's gonna have to . . . Yeah, the works – know what I mean? . . . Chuck him over? Too bloody . . .*'

I was out of there and up the street, laughing like a chimpanzee. I still had money in my pocket, I had a new dress that had cost me nothing, and Swish was down eighteen pounds. All because a girl's boyfriend didn't show.

Next thing I knew, I was outside a big department store. I went in and up the escalators to put the dress on in the toilets. I had to wriggle to get the zip up at the back. The place stank and the lights made you look like the undead. Miko used to say that guilt follows you around like a bad smell, but I didn't smell guilt in there, just old-lady perfume. And when I looked in the mirror I didn't look half bad. Sorry, *Solace* didn't look half bad. The colours went with the blonde wig and you could see her slim-slam hips. I folded the jeans and top into the lizard. *You're dead, Holly Hogan,* I said to the mirror. They can look for Holly Hogan up and down the country and they won't find her because she doesn't exist any more. *You can call me Solace from now on,* I said to my reflection.

But the dress didn't look right with trainers and socks. So I got this crazy see-through lift down to the ground floor again. I stood with my nose to where the doors open, and when it started my stomach nearly got left behind, like it used to in the sky-house lifts, and I couldn't breathe. I swear I could feel Mam gripping my shoulder. *Jeez, Holl.* In the sky house we were on the top floor, number twelve. There were two lifts, one to the even floors and one to the odd. So when the even was busy you got the odd one to floor eleven and walked the last flight. And the lifts were metal and stank of pee and Mam hated them. *I'd rather be in my own coffin than this contraption,* Holl, she'd say.

I nearly fell out when the see-through lift landed with a jerk, I was that glad to be back on solid ground. I went out and prowled around the Oxford streets some more and found a charity shop.

Grace says people who shop in charity shops are goons and look like tents. Which would make Fiona a big top, because she can't pass a charity shop without going in. Grace only likes things brand new. But I go in charity places when no one's looking and sometimes I buy a two-quid T-shirt. I didn't mean to steal this time. Not from a charity shop. Even care-babes have standards. But I went in and found black sandals my size. The heels were big chunks, three inches. And they were a fiver. One quid more than I had. I looked about. These two old mogits who ran the place were nattering on about the tennis soon starting up. *Hwim-ball-dorn-lorn-tinnis,* they said. So I ambled over to the door with the sandals in my hand like I was checking out the weather. I stood by a book-stand, pretending to read the titles. I switched the sandals from one hand to the other, so they couldn't see them from the counter. Then I drifted out the door.

'Bye,' one of the mogit ladies called.

81

I waved with my free hand and breezed down the street, swinging the sandals by their straps.

But now the bad smell Miko said about was following me round big time on account of having stolen from charity. So I crossed fast through these big yellow buildings and found a lawn by a church and it had a stone bench. I sat down and changed my shoes. I stood up and nearly fell over. I took a few steps, taller than I'd ever been before. Maybe one day I'd grow some more inches and with the heels on I'd be able to look Miko straight in the eye. Then I remembered he'd gone for good, over the river. I sat back on the bench. I still had my money and I was starving. We'd just read in class how Jane Eyre's too proud to beg and eats cold porridge out of a pig's trough. How sad is that. I'd enough for a Big Mac and some, and after I'd eaten that I'd find a bus. I'd get out of town, and I'd be heading west in my fancy new clothes.

I bought my burger and fries and ate them on a different bench, this weirdo one on the main street – you were half sitting, half leaning on it. Some freak had come up with the design just to be different. Definitely too many Es. It made your back ache.

Then the sky clouded over and it started spitting. The last fry was gone and I was still hungry and I was being jostled by people rushing past, putting up umbrellas.

Oh, God. I had nowhere to go. I had no idea where the A40 was. And I only had two quid and some change left. It wasn't even enough to buy an umbrella.

This town with the bikes and bat-wings was doing me in.

Everyone rushed past without seeing me.

The next thing I could feel a dribble of water on my mouth and I knew it wasn't rain because it tasted salty. *Get a grip,* I told myself. I got off the freako bench and staggered up the street in the heels. I thought of going back to that church place because I reckoned you could at least go and sit inside and they wouldn't charge you. But I must have turned wrong because I kept walking and couldn't find it. There was just this long road with huge trees. The drizzle got harder. Then a big building with frilly windows loomed up, set back from the road across a lawn. A notice said it was a museum and free.

Museums and me don't go. All that junk in glass cases gives me a headache, big time. But the rain was hammering down now, and the wig would be ruined if I didn't shelter. So I stumbled over and went inside.

Fifteen

The Place of Dead Things

A heavy wooden door opened into a big bright hall with white light and dinosaurs. Way overhead there was a pointed roof of metal and glass. It was hot and hushed. School kids scooted in the aisles.

I groaned. There were dead things in cases everywhere. Owls. An ostrich. A fox. Somebody had killed and stuffed them and it's mean. They should let dead things rot in the ground like they're supposed to. An otter with big dark eyes pattered across a pretend backdrop of undergrowth and water, like he was still alive. I imagined him rootling round, snuffing out his grub and taking a dip, and then somebody'd come up and coshed him on the head like they do seals in the Arctic. It's cruel.

I stopped in front of some dead old dinosaur. It was massive and had a thumb spike to kill its enemies. What would the world be like, I thought, if humans had lethal thumb spikes like that? Probably everyone would kill off everyone else and the last person would die of old age with nobody to have kids with. Then maybe the otters and seals would scamper to their heart's content and not get coshed and the world would be a better place.

Next I saw a booth with a curtain for a door. FLUORESCENT MINERALS, the sign said. Behind the curtain it was dark, with a load of rocks, and you pressed buttons to make a light come on. The rocks were dead, like everything else in the museum, but they were pretty as jewels, and jewels are things I love. Milk-white. Mauve. Silver. And amber, like my mam's ring. I thought how you'd dig them out of the ground and make million-dollar pendants out of them and walk around wowing the world, especially if you were Gorgeous Grace. I could have stared at those rocks for hours, only just after I went in, a bunch of kids shoved in behind me. They didn't bother with the rocks, though, they just kept ducking in and out, playing with the lights. All except this one serious-looking boy with round glasses. He came up as high as my elbow and had his nose glued to the glass case, reading. The other kids soon got bored and vanished, but he stayed put. We peered at the rocks together.

'They're cool, these rocks,' I said. 'Don't you think?'

'They look like they're from outer space,' he said. He was eight maybe, and already he had the same accent as Chloe and those mogits at the charity shop.

'Oh yeah?' I said. 'Says here, this one's from Iceland.'

'Maybe it came down on a meteorite.'

'Never.'

'Yes.' He turned his specs to me and his eyes were magnified through the glass. 'We're all from outer space originally,' he went. 'Every last atom inside us. We came out of a Big Bang.'

I grinned. 'Too right we did.'

'There's no such thing as aliens,' he said. 'Because, you see, we're *all* alien.' He sounded like he was lecturing a room of students with his posh, almost grown-up voice.

'If we're all alien, then there *is* such a thing as aliens,' I said.

His chin cocked like his thoughts were too big for his brain. 'Either everything's alien or nothing's alien,' he said. 'And if everything's alien then there's nothing for it to be alien against.'

'Cor.' In ten years he'd be bat-winging across Oxford, winning genius prizes by the truck-load. 'Say, I get you,' I said. 'That's wows-ville.' Wows-ville is Trim's word for when something's A-1.

The boy looked up and gave me a big smile. 'Do you really think so?' he said.

Then Junior Einstein went all shy on me again, like he'd just remembered he wasn't meant to talk to strangers, and he peered through the glass like his life depended on it. So I left him to it and went out of the cubicle, half grinning, half thinking that was one sweet boy, only he needed serious rescuing from mogitdom.

The daylight hurt my eyes. I walked past an elephant skeleton to another doorway. There was this whole other part behind, dark and crammed in with things. I went round half floating, like I do at school. You look but don't look. You switch off your thoughts and stare and think of nothing, just airwaves and bubbles. It gets right up the pit-miseries' noses. But however hard I tried, I couldn't help seeing into the cases – the spiky writing on the labels and things that looked like they belonged in the dump. One cabinet had old rope in it, no kidding. A museum where they display rope is sad.

There were totem poles, masks and mummy cases. And under the displays, the cabinets had drawers, and some you could open. I found a case with magic stuff in it, only it all looked battered and mouldering. I opened a drawer and inside was a brown beeswax model of a naked man with pins sticking out of his eyes. Yikes. Voodoo. How sick is that. I thought I'd throw up. I wouldn't do that to my worst enemy. Not even the Kavanagh kid that tore up Mam's picture. Nobody. I slammed the drawer shut, fast.

Then I came face to face with the mask. It had big empty eyes and thin cheeks. Around the edge it had curly black pretend hair, all frizzled up like some crazed doll. It was the spitting image of Denny-boy. I staggered back the way I'd come, through all the cabinets. I was dizzy, with dots fizzing round me like the air was made of lemonade. White streaks flashed across my eyelids.

Throbbing.

People.

Echoes.

Skulls.

87

I found a sign for the ladies and locked myself in. I sat down and took the wig off. I doubled over with a bad belly. I pressed my knuckles up to my eyes but all I could see was the mask face with the crazy doll-hair. It had come alive and turned into Denny-boy, the nightmare man, coming and going in the sky house, spelling trouble in both directions.

And I remembered him like it was yesterday. How his head forever knocked the paper-globe lampshade overhead. How he'd have his cut-off denim shorts on and a thick tartan shirt, like it was summer from the waist down and winter above. His hair was like a thousand corkscrews, coal-black, and his eyes bright ink-blue. He'd stand, not sit, and horse his way through a cereal bowl with the Krispies and Shreddies mixed up, shovelling them down like there was a gun to his head. Then he'd line up two thin white papers on the table and put the inside of a cigarette along it like a snake. Maybe he'd catch me looking at him and wink. 'Hey there, Holl,' he'd go. 'What are you today? Doll or troll?' I'd stare. But coming up behind me, from her bedroom, I could hear Mam's voice, laughing. 'Definitely troll today, Denny. No doll anywhere. Scram, Holl. Chop-chop. Tell Colette's mam downstairs to take you to school. I'm a wrecked woman.'

Someone was hammering on the door to the ladies. '*All out, all out. Museum's closing in two minutes.*'

I looked up at my lizard-skin bag, dangling from the hook on the toilet door. 'I'm a doll, Mam. A doll,' I whispered. 'Not a troll. Honest.' But Denny's face and Mam's voice had faded from my head and the sky house was gone. I was back to the present. Oxford. On the run.

I shook myself and reached for my mobile phone to see the time. Five o'clock. I couldn't believe it. The afternoon had gone and I was no closer to finding the A40. Fiona would be home in an hour and she'd find the note. It would be official. She'd call Rachel and the social services and the police. Holly Hogan's done another runner.

I stroked the wig on my lap. Nobody could catch the old Holly Hogan in that. *You keep going*, I told myself. *Under your own steam, remember? Ireland.* I'd hitch, steal money, whatever I had to do, but I'd keep going.

So I put the wig back on, brushed it down at the mirror over the sink and splashed some water on my face. Then I stepped back into the hall with the dinosaurs. There was nobody left but a guard. He gave me a piercing look like I was a prime suspect and for a minute I thought he was going to grab me, but then he smiled.

'Shake a leg,' he said, motioning towards the door.

As I cruised past him, I remembered the time in the Girl Guides when I was a kid back in the Kavanagh days, how we'd camped in the Science Museum. How daft was that? I'd gone to sleep under a pretend astronaut. Maybe, I thought, I should have taken a leaf from those Guides and stayed locked in the toilet. I'd have had a perfect place to spend the night and keep dry. I could even have raided the donations box near the main door. Then I thought of the brown wax man with pins in his eyes, the mask that looked like Denny-boy, and the sad otter that someone coshed, and I thought, No. I'd rather be out on the streets. Anywhere but here. And I've a road to find, remember? The road to Ireland.

So I trotted past the donations box, through the heavy wooden door and back out into the cool air. It was dry. There was steam coming up from the grass. The trees were rinsed green and fresh. I breathed long and deep and smiled. I'd missed the downpour and the dead things were behind me.

Sixteen

Hin-so-fish-shent Cree-dit

I was back to my glamorous Solace self. I breezed down the street, my spine straight. The only thing was, I was hungry again and cash was low. And where was the A40 and how did I get there?

I found my way back to the shops. They were closing. I made out a sandwich bar and went in.

'Can I have one?' I said to the girl. 'For free, like?' Trim told me he got food from shops at the fag-end of the day for nothing because else it just goes in the bin.

The girl looked at her fingernails. 'What makes you think we do that?' she drawled.

'End of the day, maybe?'

'We keep our sandwiches over for tomorrow, here.'

'Never.'

''S not up to me. It's policy. Courtesy of the manager.' She stared at her fingernails some more.

'Nice nail polish,' I said.

'It's Arctic Green.'

''S pretty. Cool, like peppermint.'

'You hungry?'

'Tell me about it.'

'You skint?'

'Tell me more about it.'

'Take one, then. The chicken mayo and avocado's my favourite.'

I grinned and helped myself. 'Ta a lot. My name's Solace, by the way.'

'Solace?' The girl handed me a napkin.

'Yeah.'

'Never heard that name before.'

'No. I was named after a horse.'

'A horse?'

'Yeah. A racehorse.'

'Wow.'

'My mam and her boyfriend owned a stable, see. It was in Ireland with meadows and a paddock 'n' all. Mam did the training and he was the jockey. And they had this one horse.'

'Solace?'

'*Sister* Solace. And she won every single race. We made a packet.'

'Cool.'

'Yeah. And then Denny – that was Mam's boyfriend – he goes and gambles it all away. So here I am. In England. And skint.'

The girl giggled. 'Sorry.'

'Yeah. Thanks. What's *your* name, by the way?'

'Kim.'

'Say, Kim, d'you know where the A40 is?'

'Hey?'

'You know. The road that goes to Wales?' Kim stared like I'd asked the way to the stars. 'Never mind. Ta 'n' all for the sandwich. So long.'

'Hey, Solace,' Kim called after me.

'What?'

'I'm off clubbing later. Maybe see you there?'

'Where's there?'

'The Clone Zone. The new place. Where else?'

'Oh, yeah. I've heard of it. But being skint 'n' all—'

'Girls go free on Mondays. Up to eleven.'

'Really?'

'Yeah.'

'Maybe see you there, then.'

I walked out of the shop and over to the freako bench where you can't really sit and bolted the sandwich down. I don't know when avocado tasted so good. The bells of the city started up. I got out the map and looked up where I was. The A40 snaked across the top bit of Oxford and then westwards and the first place after Oxford was Witney. So if I got the bus to Witney, I'd be on my way. All I had to do was go back to the bus square and catch it.

I got up and walked what I thought was the right way. Instead I ended up back at the square where the church was and hobbled over the cobblestones to this round yellow dome. I peered in the windows while the bells kept jangling as if the whole city was getting married. Inside the dome were little orange desk lamps and people reading. They might as well have lived on Pluto, the way they hunched over their books. It was bat-wing paradise.

I don't know what got into me, but I got my mobile out and started dialling Fiona's number without really thinking. A recorded voice came on, another one with a posh accent.

'You have insufficient credit to make this call,' she said. *Hin-so-fish-shent cree-dit.* She made it sound like a crime.

The bell-ringings went mad.

The nail bomb in my head was about to blow.

Hin-so-fish-shent. It was like the woman was predicting my fate. I switched off the phone and buried it at the bottom of the lizard. I went away from the bells, up a narrow street with vans parked and old cardboard boxes everywhere. '*Big Issue, Big Issue,*' this guy was bawling halfway down. He was more my type, I thought. Not like those bat-wings in the fancy round building. He had piercings in his ears and nose and cheeks and lips and probably his tongue. Grace called those types 'magnet people'. You can't possibly be a mogit if you're a magnet person. Grace wanted a stud in her tongue something desperate, only she was too chicken to get it done and I wouldn't go with her because it would've made me sick to see it. This guy had enough metal in him to sink the *Titanic.*

'Roll up, roll up,' Magnet Man yelled. '*Big Issue?*' he went, holding out a newspaper that looked like it had been through a million grubby hands.

'No thanks.'

He grinned. He had gaps between his teeth you could drive a car through. It reminded me of Colette, this girl I knew in the sky house. She lived two floors

94

down and we played broken dollies on the scary stairs, dropping them crash-hard down, far as we could. Half Colette's teeth had fallen out. Or maybe they'd never grown in the first place.

'Aw, go on, take it,' Magnet Man said. 'It's my last one.'

'Would if I could,' I said. 'But I'm cash-free.'

'Cash-free?'

'Skint.'

'You can't be skinter than me, honey. Not with those clothes.'

He had holes in his trousers and his T-shirt looked like it had been buried and dug up again. I smiled. 'D'you know where the square with all the buses is?'

'Gloucester Green?'

'Yeah.'

'I'll take you there.'

'No need. Just point me.'

'It's kind of wibbly-wobbly.' His fingers did a flickery thing under my nose.

'OK. You lead. I'll follow.'

He started off up the street. Every ten metres he turned to grin like a deranged fish. 'What d'you think of Oxford?' he said.

'Crap-ville.'

'Too right. Where you from?'

'Hampstead Heath,' I said.

'Nah. Never.'

'It's true. What about you?'

'Place called Dudley.' He said Dudley like it was Planet Paradise.

'That explains it,' I laughed.

'Explains what?'

'It's where duds come from, right?'

He turned and wagged a finger at me. 'Not duds,' he said. 'Dudes. Every last one of us.'

'OK. Dudes it is.' I smiled. 'Cool dudes.'

He grinned back. Then he kept on down the road. We crossed streets and turned corners and passed a cinema. Finally we stopped at the corner of the square. The roar of the buses was deafening.

'Here y'are,' said Magnet Man.

I looked at his rough stubble and thought if he shaved and brushed up he might be nearly cute. 'Ta 'n' all,' I said.

'Where are you off to?' he asked.

'London. Going clubbing.'

'Thought you was skint.'

'The boyfriend's paying.'

'*The boyfriend's paying*,' he repeated in a fruity voice. 'All right for some. We can't *all* wear dresses like yours.'

I smoothed down the rose and mint-green clouds. 'D'you like it?'

'You look like a supermodel, darlin'.'

No one had ever told me that before. Grace said I badly needed to lose ten pounds, get hair-thickener and stretch my neck. Trim said I looked all right in the right light. I grinned at the magnet man and he laughed. So I leaned over and whispered, 'I nicked it.'

'Way to go, girl,' he said. 'Wick-ed.'

'Ta-ra-la, so,' I said. I did a royal wave with my wrist

96

spiralling and he drifted off back the way we'd come.

I wandered round the square until I saw a man selling tickets. I didn't like approaching officials but I figured Solace was safe. I asked him how to get a bus to Witney and he said it wasn't from the square but somewhere else I'd never heard of. So I said where was that and he started saying it was down and around and right and left and my eyes glazed over, so then I asked how much was the fare and he said it wasn't his bus company but he'd guess about four quid.

Which left me snookered.

Hin-so-fish-shent cree-dit.

Seventeen

Safe in the Dark

Oxford was starting to feel like glue. I remembered Miko saying how when he hitched rides on the road he tried never to get set down in a big city because getting out again is a pain and was he right.

It would be night soon and where would that leave me?

I left the square and walked around and that's when I saw the Clone Zone. It took up half a street and it was shut. I looked in the door but the place was dead. It was too early. A sign said it opened at eight thirty.

Then I had my idea.

I'd cruise out the night in Oxford and hit the road again in the morning. For now, I'd maybe take in a movie, then the club, since girls went free tonight, and have a blast. I'd never been clubbing before on account of looking too young. But as Solace, I reckoned I could blag my way in anywhere. Who knows? Maybe I'd meet some guy with a sports car who'd drive me halfway to Fishguard. Or maybe Kim and I would get together at the club and she'd have a car and together we'd drive up a storm.

In my dreams. But at least indoors I'd be safe and dry, not alone out there in the dark streets with lunatics, drug addicts and axe murderers. Not to mention the police, prowling around, waiting to pick you up and slam you in a cell.

I headed back towards the cinema I'd passed earlier and drifted in.

There's this trick Trim, Grace and I did to see a free film. You check out a screen where the show's already started. By then they've given up on checking tickets. You cruise in. If anyone stops you, you say you had to use the toilet and your mate's got the tickets. But they hardly ever do.

So I slipped in and sat down in front of this big screen, only the seats were not even one-tenth full. And no wonder. The film was a turkey, flat out.

I'd have preferred *Titanic* any day.

Eighteen

The Clone Zone

When the lights came up, I yawned and strolled out into the evening. The air smelled of Indian food, and people lounged round like the night would never come. As for the Clone Zone, it was a whole different story. Men in suits and shades stood at the door like they were robots protecting their space rocket. A queue had formed and the doors were open. Boys – some shrimps, some big – and girls – loads of them, in tight tops – nattered non-stop. The place was high with ten types of perfume.

I was in business.

I parked behind a gang of ten screeching like they were already inside drowning out the music. I let the lizard slip halfway down my arm to look more casual. I stuck out like Dumbo the Elephant with nobody to talk to. I stood in line and counted my fingernails. Then I remembered the mobile. I could always *pretend* I had credit. I could always *pretend* Grace or Trim was on the other end. So I got it out, switched it on, and started nattering into it big time.

'Yeah, Grace,' I crooned. 'Flat-out gorgeous . . . What's that? . . . Yeah. Too right . . . Ireland. Yep. That's where I'm headed. Mam's waiting. She's got me this dancing job, all lined up . . . You'd better believe it, hon, because—' A beep on the phone interrupted me. Voicemail. So I pressed 1 and Fiona's voice started up.

'*Holly. Holly? Where are you? I just got back. I just found the note, Holly. I don't know what this is all about. Please ring me. I'll try again in ten minutes and then, well, I'll have to phone Rachel, Holly. Please ring me. I'm sorry I was late, I—*'

I didn't listen to any more. I threw the phone back in my bag like a hot coal. I whistled through my teeth and the line started moving.

I shook my head to get Fiona out of it, only her bleating voice was like a bad sofa-spring digging into me.

Close to the doors, I got nervous. I remembered the time I'd gone clubbing with Grace and Trim and had to run. Grace got in because she was five foot nine, then Trim did because they were short of boys, but I'm just average height and a girl, so the bouncer asked me for proof of my age and I had to scram. Grace was wild. She didn't want to go in with just Trim on account of Trim acting like a head-case. So she ditched out, then Trim did. That was the night we raised hell on the street instead and I landed in the secure unit and it was all that bouncer's fault.

When I got to the front this time, one of the clones raised his shades and stared at me. I knew not to look away. I stroked the ash-blonde locks and smiled. He nodded and waved the gang in and me too, thinking I was with them. The boys stopped at a ticket booth to pay but not the girls. They breezed through like they owned the place and I coasted along with them, a grin from ear to ear that I'd made it. Another clone thrust me a card.

PRESENT THIS AT THE BAR FOR YOUR FREE DRINK

Being a slim-slam girl really got you places.

Inside, it was a factory. The music thudded like heavy machinery. The ceiling was low-slung with pipes and wires, and two searchlights swooped the space. An empty dance floor winked with different colours, lit from below. It had squares of red, black, blue, yellow, and never two together, like the house doors on Mercutia Road. The bar was sleek and silver with mauve lights and upside-down bottles. Men in black vests hip-hopped behind, pouring things out for a line of girls. The sofas near it were covered with zebra-stripe fabric.

I looked around and cruised to the bar.

I knew what to ask for. Grace told me about this shot called Baby Guinness. It looks like Guinness, but it's actually coffee liqueur and Baileys. It's dark and creamy and Grace said she liked it because it's sweet and black like her and I wanted it, because I'm Irish and Guinness is our national drink.

I put in the order and the guy went to it.

'Some speed,' I yelled.

He grinned. 'Simple when you know *how*,' he bellowed. He made a Baileys bottle do a somersault on '*how*' at the same time as he sent a glass flying through the air from one hand to the other.

'Fab!' I shouted.

The barman twizzled round and pushed the drink across the bar and waved me on. Know what? I still had the card for the free drink. I walked away and cackled through the R & B beat. Then I nearly dropped the drink when a searchlight landed on me. I froze like an escaped prisoner. And that's what I was, a prisoner on the run. I scurried to a corner table out of the searchlight's path. The sandals were like animal traps cutting into my feet, so I sat down. I checked out the wig tabs. I meant to make the drink last but instead I kept sipping so as not to seem a spare wheel. The liquid went down, black, thick, cool, frothing up on my top lip. I licked it off.

Your name's made out of cloud, Holly.

I looked around. Nothing. It was Ray's voice, echoing in my head, not the club. I put my hands to my ears to drown it out.

The voice didn't come again, but through the thumpety-thud of the beat I swore I heard my mobile doing its Arabian Nights tune from the bottom of my bag. Ray or Fiona. Bound to be.

I got the thing out and, sure enough, Fiona's name was on the display. This time I turned the phone off, opened it up and took the SIM card out, then put it all in the lizard and downed the last of my drink in one.

And I thought how maybe I'd flog the phone first chance and get some money together and hit the road again.

Then I went up and got another Baby Guinness from a different barman. I fluttered my eyelashes at him as hard as I could, but this time he made me hand the card over.

I sat down. Not a soul came close. It was thin on the ground, just patches of people and nobody dancing except some crazed guy with a downy goatee who thought he was top of the pops. His mates were jeering as he scissored and spun. He didn't care. I kept at the drink, nodding to the beat. A hot hum was in my head. When I'd done, I decided I needed a once-over. I went down these steep steps with orange banisters. There were two doors – ladies and gents, I guessed, but there was nothing to say, only weird photos of fruit. One was a banana, the other an apple, halved.

Just then a girl came out of the apple door, so I went in. There was a long mirror with fancy lights, the kind Mam would have had in her dressing room at the club where she danced. They made me feel like a movie star. I brushed up and glossed down.

Then two girls barged in.

'It's him. He's just walked past without saying *nothing*,' one panted.

'Yeah. So?' drawled the other.

I froze.

'He's a bastard.'

It was the girl from Swish! I was in the mint-green

104

and rose dress and she'd see it and know right off I was the robber.

She dumped her bag down and got out her make-up. 'I'll kill the sod,' she hissed. She smacked on the lipstick and snarled.

I'd be safe upstairs in the dark and flashing lights. I whisked past her with my back turned and got out the door fast.

By the time I got to the top of the stairs, I'd calmed down. If the girl spotted the dress, I could always say I'd been given it by a friend. But she probably wouldn't spot me. It was dark and it was hotting up. I'd be lost in the crowd.

I went over to check the lizard in. It cost a pound, but what else could I do? It was too heavy to dance with. The goatee guy on the dance floor had been joined by dozens of others. I stood at the edge and wiggled my hips. A zigzag light flickered, showing up the white in everyone – their clothes, their teeth, their underwear. Then a gang like a tidal wave carried me with them onto the dance floor. I knew the tune, so I turned and grooved and did my mini palm-dives which Grace said were cool and Trim said made me look like an Egyptian mummy that's been on the Breezers. Halfway through I felt a hard nip on my behind. I spun round. Whoever had done it had gone.

Then they played this mad cover of Mam's favourite song, 'Sweet Dreams (Are Made Of This)', and the whole place took off. But after a while the beat stumbled and slowed and fell into a song about marimbas and mojitos, and you were supposed to shake out your hips like you were wearing a grass skirt. It was calypso time. The crazed dude with the goatee came up and danced with me. He'd planted a cocktail umbrella behind his ear. He reminded me of Trim so I danced back and another hit came on.

'It's a *blast*,' he yelled.

I smiled and wagged a finger at him like he was a bad dog and he jumped in the air like a firecracker. He'd a grin the size of a rolling pin when he landed.

'Wanna drink?' he roared.

'Yeah, ta,' I shrieked.

He got me by the elbow and snaked me through the flying limbs. The place was heaving.

He got a shot and passed it over. It was purple and smelled like HP sauce.

'What's that?' I yelled.

'It's a Deathwish,' he went.

I took a sip and gagged. It tasted of liquorice, bitter-sweet. ''S not bad.'

'You gotta knock it back.'

So I did. Then I took the cocktail umbrella out of his ear and twirled it. 'What's your name?'

'Ryan,' he yelled.

'Sounds Irish.'

''S not really. My mum lives in Basingstoke.'

'Mine *is* in Ireland.'

Maybe he didn't hear. He said, 'Crowded, right?'

'Yeah. Packed to the rafters.' I looked up at the weird pipes on the ceiling. 'Only there aren't none.'

'What?'

'Rafters. There aren't none.'

He looked at me like I was a head-case.

'Name's Solace,' I said.

'Alice?'

'Nah. *Solace*. Like *comfort*.'

'You wanna Southern Comfort?'

'Yeah. Whatever.' He bought it and I knocked it back. 'D'you need a mobile phone?' I screamed.

'What?'

'A mobile. D'you need one?'

'You're one crazy girl. I've got one already. Hey. Dance another?'

'Sure thing.'

We had to get round this girl who'd fallen flat on the floor. We sashayed into the middle with me doing the mini palm-dives and the dark figures coming up close and going away, like in a swimming pool. It was *swoosh-swoosh*, Ryan and me, with the arms flying, and we were spinning and it was like bells ringing and confetti flying and sweet dreams were made of this. I was alive, floating, swooping the squares under my feet song after song like the night was for ever and I was happy, I was flying, I was Solace to the power of ten.

Nineteen

The One-eyed Horror Story

The beat, the heat. Limbs and hair. ' 'S more like it,'
someone said up close. A breathy voice. An arm on
my shoulder. It went down my back and when I
opened my eyes it wasn't Ryan but some other bloke
I hadn't realized I'd been dancing with. Where was
I? I felt like I'd been dancing for ever and couldn't
remember what had happened to Ryan. This one
was eyeball to eyeball with me, only one of his eyes
was covered over with a patch, just like a pirate.
He had sweat in the pores on his nose and his
hand was on my bum like he owned it. I jumped
back.

'Gotta go,' I said, running off the dance floor
to the ladies. The place lurched and picked up
speed. I got to the banisters and I went down,
clomp-clomp, and when I got to the toilets I nearly
went in the banana door but remembered just
in time. I shut myself in a cubicle and put my
head on my lap and it felt bad. The world
flipped. My ears fizzed and a plane in my stomach

nose-dived. I turned and threw up into the toilet bowl.

That felt better.

Grace is always throwing up her food and says you feel great after. I'd never believed her but now I did. I could breathe again.

I came out and washed my face at the sink. My cheeks cooled off. Down the line, some girls were doing their mascara and chatting so I asked them the time. I couldn't believe it when they said two. Where had the hours gone?

I drifted back upstairs. I didn't know what to do. I didn't want to go on my own into the dark night outside.

'D'you wanna dance or what?' I turned round to find that same guy again. I looked to see if Ryan was around but couldn't spot him. Then I remembered Kim from the sandwich shop but she hadn't shown all night. So much for my plan that she and I'd drive up a storm. The place was thinning out. This guy had on a red T-shirt that said MADE IN ENGLAND. He had a stubbly chin and black hair scooped back and shiny. He was tall and what Grace would call raunchy. And his eye-patch nearly killed me.

'Need a drink first.'

'OK. Let's get one.'

He got me a Bacardi Breezer without asking. When I'd glugged it back we hit the dance floor, only this time I kept hopping back when he got too close.

' 'S late,' he bellowed.

'Yeah.'

'Very.'

'Yeah.'

'D'you wanna come back to my place or not?'

'Huh?' I pretended not to hear although his mouth was nearly down my ear.

'My place. It's not far.'

'Where not far?'

'It's west Oxford, Dean Court.'

'*West* Oxford?'

'Yeah.'

'Is that near the A40?'

'Kind of. The A40's a mile or two down the road. Why?'

'Just curious.'

'D'you wanna come or not, Miss Curious?'

'Have you got wheels?' I said.

'Nah. We'll get a cab.'

Well, what would *you* have done? I was wrecked. My feet were killing me. My stomach hurt. What was the choice? Park down on a bench for the night and get caught by the police or cruise off westwards in a cab?

'OK,' I said.

Grace came into my head. *Men. Use 'em and lose 'em.*

'What d'you say your name was?' the man asked.

'Solace.'

'Mine's Tony.'

'Hello, Tony.'

He grabbed my arm and swept me out the door.

He was in such a hurry I nearly forgot the lizard. But I wasn't a dimwit, not like Jane Eyre. *She* left her trunk on the carriage when she ran off. She was one Jane Airhead. *I* remembered just in time. The cloakroom ticket was where I'd stashed it. Down my bra.

Twenty

Tony's Place

Outside it was dark and warm and the streets were
silent. Tony kept walking on down an endless road,
steering me by the elbow, then I stumbled and
moaned about my feet and a cab appeared and we got
in. I think my brain switched off. I don't remember
him or me saying a word on that back seat, only my
feet and head being mashed and the night going by
and me wishing we could stay driving in that cab for
ever, driving west, with the morning catching us up
and Oxford being left behind and Ireland getting
closer every mile. I liked the lampposts swooshing past
and the smell of the leather seats and the quiet.

But the drive ended. Tony told the driver to pull up
and paid and led me through a front door. We went into
a hallway that smelled of someone's bad old stew. He
went 'Shush!' and took me to a room upstairs. He shut
the door softly after us and switched on the light.

There were beer-cans on the floor and a lumpy
sofa and a huge TV and a bed in the corner.

I flopped on the sofa.

'Make yourself at home,' he said.

I felt like passing out.

'D'you want a drink?'

'Sure.'

He rooted in a cupboard. 'There's only one left.' He held up a beer.

'You have it,' I said. I tried my royal wrist wave but the motion made my stomach somersault.

He opened it and it fizzed onto the back of his hairy hand. 'D'you wanna watch TV?'

'TV?'

'Or a film. I have a few.' I had this image of him putting on loads of porn. 'I've got all the *Terminators*,' he said.

'*Terminators?*'

His Adam's apple bulged as he knocked back the beer. 'Not your thing?'

The room spun.

'Yeah, sure,' I said. 'Let's watch one.'

He put a DVD on and sat down next to me on the sofa. He switched it on with the remote. I kept drifting off but every so often sudden clanking sounds would wake me up and make my head pound.

After this bit where a man got a big metal stake driven through him, Tony laughed and switched it off. 'That's the funny part over. The rest's boring.'

'Oh. Sure.'

'Maybe you just wanna lie down?'

We were coming right down to it. *Use 'em and lose 'em*, Grace crooned in my head.

'Lie down?' I croaked. Fact is, I'd not done sex yet.

Grace had, millions of times, and Trim. So he said. But not me. Grace said how it's no great shakes, you just shut your eyes and dream of ice cream, and if you play your cards right, they pay you something. But I wasn't sure about this guy.

He lit a fag without offering me one. 'Bed,' he said. He nodded over to the stripy duvet cover that made my head whirl just looking at it.

'You mean, like, sleeping 'n' all?'

He looked at me sprawled on the sofa and blew out a smoke ring. 'Hell with sleeping.'

Jeez. How do I get out of this one?

'About your eye,' I said, trying to change tack. 'What's wrong with it?'

He fingered the patch and laughed. 'Got into a fight,' he said.

'Who with?'

'My girlfriend.'

'Your *girlfriend?*' I looked around like maybe she was hiding in a cupboard.

'*Ex*-girlfriend.' He gulped the last of the beer and leaned towards me. 'Definitely ex.' I froze. He tickled my kneecap. 'Ex,' he murmured.

Don't just sit there. Do something.

He had a hand round the back of my neck. The other went ferreting over my dress, the fag hanging out limp between his fingers.

'Youch! Watch your fag,' I said.

'Oh. Yeah. Sorry.' He flicked it to the floor and ground it out with his heel. Then he burped. Then he went ferreting again over the dress.

'Hey, I just remembered—' I started.

He yanked me towards him. I lurched back and the wig came off.

It toppled onto the floor by the arm of the chair, pale and floppy.

'Hell,' he swore. He shoved me away. 'What's *that?*' His voice squeaked like a choirboy's.

I gathered up my knees to my chin and said nothing.

He picked up the wig. He looked at it, then me. 'Your hair's *brown.*'

I couldn't even blink.

'I don't go for brown.'

I bit down on my lip.

'I only do blonde.'

His bleary eye was staring at me like I was an alien. 'You're just a kid, aren't you?'

I stayed curled up tight, cornered.

'Aren't you?' His hand moved as if he was about to hit me. 'Aren't you?'

I put my hands in front of my face. 'Sorry, Tony. Sorry.'

He swore under his breath. Then his hand fell to his side. He lit up another fag and dragged on it. 'Jeez-us. I don't fancy *kids.* I'm not a bloody perv. How old *are* you?'

That's when it hit me. It was three in the morning and my birthday. Some birthday present. A one-eyed horror story.

'Fifteen,' I said.

He swore again. '*Fifteen?* Christ. Get out.'

'Out?'

'Yeah. If my landlord catches you I'll be finished.'

I got up off the chair.

'Clear off,' he said. 'Go home to Mummy.'

My lip wobbled. 'I don't have no home.'

'Go find a homeless shelter then. Whatever.'

He tugged me off the chair, picked up the wig and threw it at me like it was heaving with maggots. He jerked me towards the door. 'Beat it.'

'Please, Tony,' I said. 'It's dark out there. Let me stay. I'll take my clothes off. If you want. Or I'll give you my mobile phone. For rent, like. Just let me stay on the sofa till morning. Please—'

He pushed me out and threw my lizard-skin bag after me. 'Out,' he hissed.

'Please—'

'Shush.' He shut me out on the landing.

I heard a key fumbling, then turning in a lock. '*Tony . . .*'

I stood with my nose and palms pressed to the door but it didn't open.

Outside was the night, waiting to swallow me whole.

What the hell was I supposed to do now?

Twenty-one

The Dream on the Stairs

I stood still in the strange dark house. I saw the strip of light under Tony's door and nothing else. I smelled burned stew and damp and my own fear.

I stood with the wig pressed up to my face.

In a moment my eyes adjusted. I turned round and made out the stairs, the banister, a hall table at the bottom. I crept forward and sat on the top step.

I went halfway down the stairs on my backside and stopped. I listened. There must have been a clock somewhere because I heard it over the thumping of my heart. *Tick-tock-stick-stuck.* I remembered the clock in Mercutia Road but this one wasn't the same. This one was heavy and slow.

Everything else in the house was silent.

The strip of light under Tony's door went out. And was I ever glad his girlfriend had given him a shiner. I wished I'd made the other eye shine too. Like having brown hair was a sin? I touched my own hair. After the wig I felt bald almost, and I remembered how Grace was always saying to get a perm or do something to

117

make it thicker. And I cried; the tears wouldn't stop.

There wasn't a sound from Tony's room. He must have gone to bed, thinking I'd left the house.

My eyes adjusted again. I took the sandals off and rubbed my feet. Then, quietly, I changed into my trainers and put my skater top back on over the dress. I stroked Solace, pale and limp on my lap. The ash-blonde colours glowed in the dark.

The place smelled bad but I'd be safe here for an hour or two if I kept still. 'Solace,' I whispered, like the wig was an old friend. 'Sister Solace.' *Tick-tock-stick-stuck.* Time stopped. My brain slowed and I was floating. I shut my eyes and maybe I was awake or maybe I was asleep but soon the stairs vanished and I was back in the sky house, like I'd got there on a dream cloud . . .

I'm shooting a movie underwater, looking through a wavering lens.

Mam's there. Denny too. Their voices echo and it's spring. Bright light pours in from the balcony and Denny's tapping the newspaper. He's off to the races for the day. Mam's at him to back her a horse. I remember now. It's the day of the Sister Solace race.

'I've never so much as blown in a nag's nose,' Denny's going, 'but I know my horses.' Mam pinches his cheek and flashes a fiver.

'Shall I put it on for you, Bridge?' he coaxes, trying to catch it. 'A fine strapping mare?'

'Can I choose? Can I?' That's me talking. I'm right

in there, pulling at Denny's tartan cuff on account of I only come up to his elbow.

'OK, troll. Which one?' He shows me the racing page.

I put my finger on Sister Solace. 'That one.'

'Sister Solace? She's a long shot.' He plucks Mam's fiver from her and she hands him another.

'Put them both on her,' Mam says. 'I like the sound of her name.'

'It's form you go for, you daft woman. Not the bloody name.'

Mam's laughing, ruffling his hair. 'Do as I say, Denny. Sister Solace.'

'All right, Bridge. Don't say I didn't warn you.' Then he's kissing her goodbye and he's gone and it's 'Cut to the Race'.

Mam and I are watching it on TV. The horses pound from the stalls, going for broke, the ground thundering under their hooves. Their necks stretch out and their behinds bulge with brown muscle and you can see the pale gold one, Sister Solace, straggling. Mam's cursing. Then, from nowhere, she's there, up at the front. The voice of the man who's talking over them goes up an octave – '*And it's Sister Solace on the outside, it's Sister Solace . . .*' – and Mam's standing, her fist pumping the air, and she's shouting, 'Go, girl!' So I stand and shout too and Sister Solace goes flying, pale and smooth, ahead of the rest, and it's a miracle the way she's nearing the finish, will she topple or burst, no, she's there, first past the post. Mam's jumping, saying it's champagne tonight, praise be, I'm her own best girl. And she's putting on 'Sweet Dreams (Are Made Of This)', her favourite song, and pouring her drink with the clicking ice cubes. 'To Sister Solace,' she croons. She jiggles around the sky house and opens the balcony door to let in the breeze. *Travel the world and the seven seas.* It's so clear you can see the white dome of St Paul's and I'm wriggling and jiggling alongside Mam, copying her mini palm-dives. She jives and spins and claps and so do I. I don't know when my heart felt more like a firework, bursting into a thousand golden coins.

'Is it money enough for Ireland, Mam? Is it?'

'It is, Holl. More than enough. Enough for a diamond jewel. Enough for a brand-new bed. Whatever. We're rich.'

'But will we go to Ireland, now, Mam? Will we?'

'Yes, course we will, Holl.'

And I'm imagining running in the green fields through the silky rain, breathing in pints of soft fresh air and throwing the sticks in the black river. We're off to Ireland, we are.

'Will that man ever come home, so we can see the colour of our money?' Mam croons and pours another. The sky-house lifts are whirring, coming up towards us. 'Is that him now?' Mam says. 'Is it?'

Holl. Quick.

Above me, a board creaked. I jolted awake. The sounds of the sky house vanished and I was back on those strange stairs in the small hours. I was curled higgledy-piggledy, my cheek pressed to the wig. A thin light was creeping in from the front door. I heard a footstep above me, then another.

Holl. Quick. Get. Out of here.

A door opened. There was a grunt, whether a man or a woman I wasn't sure, but in a second they'd turn the light on and I'd be caught.

I grabbed my things and scrambled down the stairs. I banged my knee against the table at the bottom.

'Hey! You!'

A man's voice, not Tony's, someone older.

I was at the front door, fumbling at knobs and handles, getting nowhere. The lights came on.

'I'll call the police!'

I got the door open and scrambled out, groaning with the bad knee.

'Stop! You!'

He was coming down after me. I forgot the knee and ran out blindly, down the path, down the street and out onto a main road and the knee-bang didn't hurt I ran so hard. I ran until I was out of breath and then some more, and then I switched to the pavement and walked again and the knee-hurt came back.

When I looked over my shoulder, nobody was following. I got my breath back. It was quiet, half dark, half light. I was by a bus shelter, so I sat down.

Everything was grey. No birds. No cars.

There were grass patches on the sides of the roads. The houses were big and more spread out. The trees didn't move. Cold air played around my nose.

I thought of the house and the smell and Tony's

roving hands and the stairs and the man who'd shouted at me and how it was my birthday and nobody knew, and I cried. I cried like I'd been caught, even though I hadn't.

Somewhere in my head, Mammy was crying right alongside me. *Travel the world and the seven seas*, she sang over her empty glass. *Everybody's looking for something.*

But Denny didn't come that day. I remembered now. No champagne, no party, no tickets to Ireland. All I could see through that cracked old movie lens was Mam's empty glass tipped over by her side and the left-over ice in it melting, and me, putting my own self to bed, crawling under the duvet with Rosabel up by my face, humming Sweet Dreams over and over. And no sign of Denny-boy anywhere.

Twenty-two

A Walk Through the Dawn

Was I a mess.

A bird started up in a bush behind me. He was chirping away for all England. I wiped my face on my sleeve.

You can't go to Ireland in this state, I told myself.

I brushed out the wig and put it on. Then I got my doll-pink lipstick out, and my little mirror. I saw hair jumbled, my own baby-fine brown showing under the blonde, and my eyes red and small nose shining. I straightened out the wig and brushed it down again. I dusted down the dress. I did the lips and dabbed the face.

Then I remembered the iPod in my bag. I put the earphones in to end the silence.

I sat there nodding to my favourite tracks. I thought of Ryan with his rolling-pin grin, then Tony with his beer-breath. I tried to put him in the trash part of my brain where you recycle things, but he kept popping back with his raunchy face and bleary one eye. And then his face was like the mask face in the museum, and then like Denny-boy's. So I turned the music up louder, but no matter how loud I played it, there he was, eye-patch and all.

Was I glad he hadn't got my dress off.

There's only one person who I'd let near me in that way and he was nowhere close. And I'm not going to talk about him.

I got myself up and walked on down the road. My back was to the dawn, so I reckoned I was heading west and west was the right way for Ireland. I walked to the soft beat of Storm Alert. It was like everyone in the world was dead except for me.

Then, over the music, I heard a slow car approaching from behind. I tensed up. Maybe the driver was checking me out. A kerb-crawler. The trouble with being an all-time slim-slam glamour girl is it gets you noticed. The car kept crawling and I walked faster. It reminded me of the night I got busted. It was after the bouncer at the club turned me away. Trim said, *Let's all go hooking.* That way we'd raise money and go gambling and end up millionaires. Grace knew all about sex. She told me her stepdad was her first boyfriend and that's what had landed her in care-babes-ville. So that night with Trim she picked up a cruiser in a shiny suit and red car straight off. She came out five minutes later with a tenner, only she wouldn't give it to Trim and he went wild and made me go hooking next. I stood on a corner, hip jutting out, tossing my head like Grace had, and a car slowed. But instead of a sex-hungry man it was the police. They stopped and took me away. They asked who I was with, but I didn't tell on Trim and Grace. I said I was working the street alone. And that's how I got sent to the secure unit and it was one bad time.

It was bad now. This car cruising alongside me wouldn't shift. I didn't look over. I started nodding my head to the music and punching the air like a mad person. Mad people and hooking don't go together, I reckoned. I hopped and poked like crazy. And you know what? It worked. The car zoomed past and away and was I glad.

So if you're *ever* bothered by a crawler, you know what to do.

Then I kept up a good pace even though my head was thumping it faster than the music. Houses. Grass. Trees. Pavement. *Thud-thud.* My head ached, my eyelids felt like sandpaper. I took the earphones out and kept going. Two cars raced past, like they were chasing. I got to an underpass. Up over a dingy bridge, traffic zoomed by in spurts. I saw a slip road leading up to it and I sat down on a grassy bank near there for a rest. It was damp with dew but I didn't care.

Grace came and sat next to me, her face and lashes long.

Some bridge, Holly.

Yeah.

Some height.

Yeah. So?

You ask me what I'd do if I were you? I'd go up there and jump.

That was Grace, always going on about topping herself. Sod off, Grace. Lemon-head.

Her long lashes vanished.

I was left on my own. I pictured going up the slip road and onto the bridge, saying goodbye to the world and leaping off. How would that feel, the dropping and the car tyres and the ground zooming up and hitting every bit of me?

My French teacher at school told this story once about this mademoiselle who was heart-broke. She goes up the Arc de Triomphe in the middle of Paris to jump off and end it all. Only she comes down on a big white van and her legs go through and she breaks them both and gets done by the van insurance for the damage and is ruined and crippled for life and not one bit dead. I remember thinking that pills and booze is the way to go if you've half a brain. Grace has tried nail scissors and starvation and got nowhere. But she doesn't even have a quarter-brain.

I stroked my wig and it was like Solace took charge. *You're not leaping off that bridge, Holl,* she said. *The wig would come off, wouldn't it? Then I'd be dead too.* I had to smile. *Just keep going up this road. Ireland will get closer every step.*

So I did. I just kept going and going into that quiet morning.

Twenty-three

The Phone Box

The houses were more spaced out.

The light was stronger.

I put the phones back in. The birds were singing fit to burst my skull. Drew was pouring words into my ear. I suppose he's the other guy, aside from the one I'd rather not mention, who I'd let near me, but he's always on tour nowhere near so we haven't had a chance to meet. One day Storm Alert will play where I am and I'll have a ticket and I'll go. And that will be the same day that terrorists burst into the stadium and keep us all hostage. Then, in the negotiations, they'll let people free, a hundred at a time, until we're down to the last ten. Drew and me'll both still be there and he'll get to know me and we'll chat up a storm. And when one of the terrorists tries to shoot dead this little kid-boy, a bit like the Junior Einstein boy in the museum, I'll jog the terrorist's trigger-hand and the boy will be safe. Only, in revenge, the terrorist will knock me out with the handle of his gun. Then, when I wake up, Drew will be cradling my head in his hands and stroking my hair . . .

I was so lost in my thoughts I nearly bumped into a phone box, the old-fashioned red kind with lots of little windows. I looked at it in a daze like I'd forgotten what it was.

Next minute I was inside, thinking who to phone. Trouble was, the whole world was asleep. Grace, Trim, asleep. Miko, in north London somewhere, asleep, and I didn't have his number. With Rachel, I'd only get her voice, recorded. I had to talk to *somebody*.

Only not Fiona or Ray. No way.

Then I remembered a phone number they posted by the phone in Templeton House. ChildLine. It's some group with a special number for us care-babes. So I thought I'd try it. It was better than nothing and it was free. I remembered its digits climbing up even, like a ladder.

But would anyone answer so early?

Brrimm-brrimm, went the phone.

I waited.

Brrimm-brrimm-brrimm. Nothing.

I nearly gave up. Then with a click a voice answered, a real voice, not recorded. Female. She came out with some patter about disclosure and confidence and I nearly hung up. A mogit, one hundred per cent.

'Are you still there?' she said. 'I haven't put you off with that official stuff?'

'Dunno,' I said.

'Well there. Hello again.'

'H'lo.'

128

'Are you a young person?'

'Yeah. Fourteen. No, fifteen.'

'Do you want to tell me your name? You don't have to if you don't want.'

'Sure. I'm Solace.'

'Solace?'

' 'S right. I'm Solace. And I'm on the run.'

There was a pause.

'I'm Gayle,' said the voice. 'Hello – Solace. I'm sorry you're running away. D'you want to talk about it?'

'Maybe. See. I was in this Home . . .' I trailed off.

'A Home?'

'Yeah. Being looked after.'

'Residential? Or fostering?'

'Residential.'

'Didn't you like it there?'

' 'S all right. Only the other kids were very naughty.' Grace and Trim were suddenly crammed up in the box with me, digging their elbows into my ribs, trying to stop up the laughter. 'Very naughty indeed.'

'I'm sorry.'

'And my key worker didn't like me. He picked on me.' Miko turned round, halfway over the river, his jacket over his shoulder. He raised a brow. *Holly.* He shook his head.

'How did he do that?'

'Dunno. Different stuff.'

'And you didn't like that?'

'Nope.'

'So you ran away?'

'Yep.'

'Don't you have a social worker, Solace? Someone who you can talk to?'

'She never answers my calls. She's too busy.'

That's what Grace says about hers. But it wasn't true of Rachel.

'So where are you running to?'

'Hey?'

'Is there somewhere you're trying to get to? Or are you just running?'

I thought of Mam in the green fields and the soft rain. 'Yeah.'

'You're just running?'

'No. I'm running – *somewhere.*'

'Do you want to tell me where?'

I couldn't stop myself. 'My mam.'

'Your mum?'

'Yeah. My mam.' I could hear my voice wobble. 'I want to go live with her. I want to be back with her. I'm tired of living with strangers.'

'Does she know, Solace? Does she know that's what you want?'

'No,' I blurted. 'She don't know nothing. Not where I am. Nothing. They don't tell her. She's looking for me. I know. She's out there, looking for me. But she can't find me.'

There was a pause.

'Solace?'

'Yeah?'

'Do you know *why* you're in care?'

I thought of the sky house and Mam and Denny. 'Oh, yeah,' I breezed. 'Sure I know.'

'Would you like to tell me about it?'

' 'S kinda complicated.'

'Try me.'

'See, Mam had this boyfriend. Denny-boy.'

'Denny-boy?'

'Yeah. He took all our money. And he did bad things. Wicked bad things. And Mam had to get back to Ireland fast so Denny wouldn't find her or she'd be dead. And they found out.'

'Who's "they", Solace?'

'Social services, of course. They found out about Mam being gone because I didn't go to school like I should have and they got onto us. Mam was going to send for me but when she did it was too late. They'd taken me away. Now she's there and I'm here and it's all my fault.'

'Why do you say it's your fault, Solace?'

'Huh?'

'Well, how old were you then?'

'Dunno. 'S a blur.'

'So you were young. Very young. You weren't responsible for whatever it was the adults did. Were you?'

You know, people always said things like: *It's not your fault, Holly. You didn't do anything wrong, Holly.* But it was like I'd never really listened before, not even to Rachel and Miko. *You weren't responsible.* Besides, they were always saying about how I should be *more* responsible, not less.

But now it was weird. The way Gayle had said it, I could feel it.

'Were you, Solace?' Her voice was soft and calm, pleading almost, and she said my name sweet. I imagined her on the other end of the line. She had pale cheeks and soft fair curls, long, and she was pretty, in a dark blue jogger with stripes down the side, not a mogit at all.

'No,' I whispered. I cradled the phone in my hand. I squeezed my eyes tight and I could see this little girl with falling-down socks and a crooked fringe and she had lots of gold stars from school and it was me, and she got the lift to the odd floors when the even lift was busy and walked up the scary stairs the last bit because she was brave. 'My money's running out,' I choked, forgetting how the call was free.

'Solace – d'you want me to phone you back?'

'No. 'S all right.'

'I can, you know.'

'Nah.'

'Solace. I have to say this. You should go back, you know.'

'Huh.'

'Will you do that? Go back. Then we can talk again. Any time you like. It's a promise. Will you?'

'Maybe,' I said.

'I don't like to think of you out on your own, this time of morning.'

'I'm not on my own.'

'No?'

'My boyfriend's with me.'

'Right. Great. What's his name?'

'Drew,' I said.

'Is he nice?'

'He's great. He's handsome. And he's looking out for me.'

'I hope so. But you must call the Home, Solace. Or I can for you, if you like. If you tell me its name.'

'The phone's counting down the seconds,' I lied. *One, two, three,* Big Ben donged in my head.

'Solace?'

Four, five.

'*Please,* Solace.'

Six, seven, eight. The voice of the Gayle woman floated inside me, right into my brain and lungs. Part of me didn't want her to go, the other part of me was frantic to hang up.

'Templeton House,' I squeaked.

Nine, ten. I heard a 'Thank—'

I slammed the receiver down. The thoughts crashed round in my head. *Jeez. What did I say that for? She'll call Templeton House and they'll realize who it was. They'll trace the call and the police will be after me. Thickhead. I'd better get on. FAST. Hot-foot.*

I came out of the phone box and looked at the road ahead. The sun had risen and the city was behind me. I hitched the lizard up onto my shoulder and ran. All I could think of was little Holly in her falling-down socks, playing broken dolls with Colette on the dark, scary stairs, begging Denny to let her choose a horse and brushing, brushing Mammy's hair for the love and the money. *You were young, Holly,* Gayle's voice kept telling me. *Very, very young.*

Twenty-four

Emmy-Lou of Eynsham Lock

You can't run for ever and soon I slowed. The morning silence was thick like soup. The houses stopped,
then the pavement. There was only a bumpy, grassy
verge. My ankles got a dew shower every step. Instead
of gardens and buildings there were fields and pylons
and trees and more green than I'd ever seen. There
were yellow and blue flowers. There were bird coos
and rustles and the smell of leaves.

And the road kept on going. More houses, then
long grass, and a field with sheep.

It was open country, nearly as pretty as Ireland,
and I could breathe. Was I glad I hadn't jumped off
that bridge, even if my belly felt like somebody was
strangling it and I was raging with thirst, and even if I
wanted to murder the birds on account of they
wouldn't shut up. But the morning was cool and alive
and calm and my feet just kept walking without me
telling them to. I imagined Mam on a hill, waiting,
watching me get closer every step.

I put two or three miles under me. Three cars and

one truck rumbled by but there was no sign of the police. Maybe I'd panicked for no reason. I hadn't said my name. But I'd said Templeton House. They'd check it out and soon put two and two together, bound to . . .

My eyes teared up but I kept walking.

Then ahead, the road went over a little bridge with an empty toll-booth. I crossed halfway and there was a blue-green sparkle either side, a river, thin and quiet. I thought of Miko crossing the Thames, heading north, miles away, in a whole other world. Then I saw a path by the water's edge and long narrow boats parked.

River water in a city is filthy, but out here I reckoned you could drink it. I stepped off the bridge and down some steps to the bank and along by the boats, trying to find a spot to lean over and scoop up a palmful.

There was a building and a wall with water pouring over it. I didn't know what the place was, but I found a spot to splash my face. The water was dark and probably full of fly eggs but I took a mouthful. It tasted like slop from a bucket when you've just washed a floor and I nearly threw up. There was a bench and I flopped down.

I saw a curl of smoke coming from one of those funny long boats and frowned.

Whoever heard of a fire on a wooden boat?

Then I heard Trim cackling at me in my head. *You can have a fire on a boat. They had them in the* Titanic *down in the engine room, right?*

Yeah, I mentally answered him. And look what happened. It sank.

Yeah, but that wasn't fire. That was an iceberg.

But these boats are tiny. Nothing like the *Titanic*. And they're made of wood. One spark and they'd be finished.

I stretched out along the bench, yawning.

You and Grace, thick as doorstops. You put the fire in something metal, stupid. Something thick and solid.

Yeah. So solid it sinks the boat? I was being deliberately thick to get his goat.

A boat could carry the Statue of Liberty if it wanted to. Depends on the size. Boat . . . like that . . . small stove . . . no problem . . . Trim's voice broke up and maybe I nodded off.

I woke up, flat out across the bench, the sun blinding my eyes.

The wig was half on, half off.

I sat up so fast it dropped off altogether. I grabbed it before it hit the ground and shoved it back on. I remembered the phone call I'd made. *The police, they're after me.* I rooted in my bag, found my brush, combed the wig and breathed. I was Solace again. No way they'd recognize me even if they passed right by.

I heard a whistling, then a splash. I looked round.

Away down the bank a man was cleaning the windows of his boat. The boat was long and green with flowerpots and a bicycle lying flat on the roof and a chimney with the smoke still rising.

The man had long grey hair tied in a ponytail and thick brown arms. He had blue jeans and a T-shirt on

136

and was whistling to a tune he could hear on his earphones. He was what I call a mogit in denial – somebody who's over forty and acts like they're seventeen. You want to cringe and hide when they act like your best buddy, like they think they're still your age.

This one stopped and took a slug out of a big bottle of posh water. It looked clear, not like the river water I'd tried earlier. My thirst raged.

I got up, dusted myself down and ambled down the bank to the boat. It was called *Emmy-Lou*, the name painted in red on the side, with a ♥ instead of the O.

'Hey!' I called.

The man didn't hear because of his music, but maybe he sensed somebody was close because he turned and caught my eye.

I waved and grinned. 'Hi,' I said.

He took out the earphones. 'Hello, there. Saw you, crashed out on that bench over there. Had a party last night?'

'Yeah. Too right. Wild.'

'How'd you end up here?'

'You really wanna know?'

'Try me.'

'I don't remember.'

'You don't remember?'

'Nope.'

'That must have been some party. How much did you knock back?'

'Don't even go there.' I put my hand to my head

like it was fancy china. 'I could use a slug of your water.'

He put his cleaning cloth down and passed me the bottle. 'Use it away.'

So I did, glug-glugging until it was empty. He watched me like I was a circus act, grinning. I passed back the bottle.

'Ta.'

'Taste good?'

'Yeah. Champagne.'

'Are you lost?' he said.

'Nah. Well, maybe a bit. I'm looking for the A40.'

'The A40? It's just a mile or two on. You hit a roundabout and turn right. What's special about the A40?'

I put a finger to my lips. 'Promise you won't tell?'

'Promise.'

'I'm meeting my boyfriend, Drew. He'll be pulled in there, waiting for me. He's picking me up in his sports car and driving me clean away. We're eloping.'

'Didn't know people did that any more.'

'They do when they're young and the parents don't approve.'

'Sounds romantic.'

'It is.' I made my eyes go starry.

'You heading to Gretna Green?'

'Hey?'

'You know. The place where people eloped to in the olden days. Clattering away in their carriages.'

'Oh, right. No. We're heading to America.'

'America?'

'Yep. By plane. Oxford, Heathrow, then take-off.'
My hand mimed a jumbo jet going up into the air.
'New York,' I added.

'America's where it's at,' he said. 'I used to live there.'

'No way. Where?'

'All over. I was a roadie.'

'A roadie?'

'I drove round with all the top bands. You name them . . .' Then he started on a list of rock legends, only I hadn't heard of any of them, they were that prehistoric. But I threw in a few *wows* like I was in awe.

'You sure you don't want breakfast first?' he said. 'I've tea brewing inside and rashers and bread.'

My insides squeezed up tight with hunger and it was like I was in 22 Mercutia Road in bed with the smell of toast coming up the stairs. His boat looked cosy, long and bright, the kind of place you could live in and never feel boxed in, and you'd have a table and cupboards to store everything away neatly and a stash of biscuits on hand and a dog like Rosabel, only real, to guard you.

'Why's she called Emmy-Lou?' I asked, to buy time.

He turned and looked at the boat's name, painted in red. 'It's after a girl I once knew,' he said, smiling.

'You loved her, right?'

'Why d'you say that?'

'You've painted a heart for the O.'

He laughed. 'Guess that settles it. Must have.'

'Did you elope with her?'

'Nah. She was in a whole other league, my Emmy-Lou.' He jerked his grey head towards the door to the inside. 'Come on in and I'll get the toast started.'

I paused, tempted. But I saw the stubble on his chin coming out white and the memory of Tony's fingers ferreting over me crawled through my head. 'Love to,' I said. 'But I've to push on or the boyfriend will be wondering.'

He nodded. 'Oh yeah. The boyfriend.'

'He's something else, Drew. If you keep him waiting he goes ballistic. But ta for the water.' Part of me was whimpering at the thought of that toast but I said goodbye and cruised back up the bank towards the bridge.

'Anytime, doll,' he called.

I looked back. *Troll or doll*, came Denny-boy's echo. But the man was waving and smiling, friendly enough, so I gave him a half-wave then walked back past the bench and up the steps. One day I'll have a green long boat just like his, I thought. Only it won't be called *Emmy-Lou*. It will be called *Solace*. And when I paint the name on the side, the letters will be bright yellow. And there'll be a red heart for the O.

S ♥ lace.

Twenty-five

The A40

Back on the road, I soon hit the roundabout sign. Off to the right was signed A40. I tramped the longest mile of all, past another roundabout, and finally hit it. The road to freedom.

I sat down on a grass verge near where the traffic slowed and got my breath back. I took out the map. I could see the road curving from one town to the next, and near a place called Eynsham there was a circle, which I put my finger on. That's where I was. Right there.

When I was on the road, Holly, I stopped near the bends. Places where a car can pull in. It was Miko's voice, retelling the story of the year he hitched from the South of France to the ferry when he was eighteen and on his own and skint like I was now. *The road, Holly,* he'd said, his eyes far away. *It rolls out ahead like the key to a mystery. You think you nearly have it but it's always one step further on. Every lift a new adventure. And the miles falling away, costing nothing.* I smiled, remembering, and changed from my trainers back into my smart sandals. Maybe they'd get me a ride faster. *It's rough being young nowadays. You can't hitch a ride any more, or play outdoors. Nor do nothing fun. All because everyone thinks everyone else is an axe murderer.*

That was Miko, that was his theme. 'The Gospel According to Miko'. He'd say how when he was a kid life was a downhill freewheel. People thumbed wherever they wanted to go and broke into empty houses to live and survived on giros from the dole office and screamed all night into a microphone and got to call it music on account of it was punk. He'd said how he used to have an earring like a silver cobra and more gashes in his trousers than material and how he'd dyed his hair green, which must be why it had all fallen out. 'You're having me on, Miko,' I said one time. 'You *shave* it off, don't you?' Somehow I was desperate for Miko's silky-smooth top to be deliberate.

He'd grinned at me: 'Sure, Holly. If I let it grow, I'd be like Rapunzel in that fairy story.' And he'd fluttered his eyelashes like he was a girl and I'd thumped him and he'd laughed and that was his way.

A lorry thundered past. I scrubbed Miko out from my brain. I stood up, grabbed the lizard, and stuck out my thumb. I knew it made me as old as the Rolling Stones but what else to do?

The cars and trucks rushed by. Nothing stopped and my arm ached.

Supposing someone stops and it's a mass murderer? I thought.

Then I thought, Mass murderers aren't exactly common as pints of milk.

I bent down and picked a dandelion from the grass and put it behind my ear. I put my thumb out again.

And you know what? A truck stopped almost at once.

It screeched to a halt on the wide verge about twenty metres down from where I was standing. Was it really stopped for *me*? I waited, feeling the wind in my ears, the sun on my shoulders. In the trees crows yattered. I held my breath.

He hooted his horn. I let out my breath.

I dusted the flower off my ear and checked the lizard.

C'mon, Holl, I told myself. *Chip-chop.*

I walked towards that truck, careful not to stumble in my heels.

If he's fat with tattoos and bristly, I'm not getting in, I thought.

Up close, I saw a hand reaching over, pushing open the passenger door. I looked up, expecting a brute with a beard and a belly plus a million tattoos. What I got was a skinny face, looking polite. There was wispy brown hair, brown eyes and smooth, baby cheeks. On his feet were open-toed sandals, which put him in the fashion year of dot.

'Where're you going?' he asked. His hands were relaxed on the wheel.

'Wales,' I said.

'You're in luck,' he said. 'I'm heading to Carmarthen.'

'Carmarthen?' I remembered the list of names

on the road and Carmarthen was far along the way.

'Any good?' he said.

'Yeah. That's great. *Really* great.'

'OK, hop in. Mind how you go.'

I climbed up. He didn't put a hand out to help, which was good. I looked for a sign of a mass-murdering mental man but couldn't find any. No guns or knives or pictures of naked ladies dangling from the mirror.

'OK?' he said. 'Name's Phil.'

He said it like a sigh. It was a soft name, not like Tony. Something about him made me feel safe. I shut the door and he revved the engine up.

'Hi, Phil.'

'What's yours?'

'Solace,' I said.

He checked his right side and pulled out. 'Solace?'

'Yeah.'

'Like hope or something?'

'That's right.'

'Never heard that before. But we could all use some.' He threw me a sad smile, then picked up speed and nodded at the seatbelt. 'Better put that on.'

'Yeah, sure.' I strapped myself in, sat back on the high seat and stared at the white dividers on the road as they sped towards us. When they started dividing up my head as well as the road, I looked out the side window over the fields.

Inside I was grinning from ear to ear. Had I hit lucky with this Phil. All I had to do was sit tight and act polite and I'd be halfway to Ireland. The police would never catch me now. As far as they were concerned, I might as well have been beamed to outer space. Carmarthen, here I come.

Twenty-six

The Vegan Truckie

For Phil, the sound of the road was conversation enough. He was like Ray, musing quietly over the wheel. The radio was on low. You could only catch snatches. What you heard most was the engine turning and the hit of the truck's fat tyres on the tarmac. I couldn't believe how high up we were in that cab, like lords of the manor. You could see over the hedges across the fields. They were dotted with purples and yellows and whites, and long lines of pylons. There were sheep and barns and houses and bends in the road that hid what was around them.

This is a breeze, I thought.

Inside the cab it felt warm and smelled of diesel. The seats were black and worn and Phil had an old green sweater hanging from a hook behind.

We came to a stretch of dual carriageway. The truck speeded up and the tyres went up a key.

'So, Solace,' said Phil. 'Haven't seen a girl hitching in a while.'

'It's legal, innit?'

'Sure is, last I heard. Just not common.'

I looked over, but his eyes were glued to the road. 'I don't hitch regular, Phil,' I explained. 'I was out clubbing last night and my money and mobile got stolen out my bag.' I pointed to the pocket of the lizard, where Mam's amber ring was stashed. 'I'm skint. And my mam's in Wales, see, and she's sick. I've got to get to her.'

'Sorry to hear that. Did you tell the police?'

'Hey?'

'About your wallet and phone?'

'Nah, no point. Whoever did it's gone off with the cash by now and thrown the wallet in the park.' I was thinking of when Trim stole that wallet on the tube. He'd dipped his hand into this lady's shopping, which was nearly up his nose in the crush. Then Trim, Grace and myself hopped off at the next stop and ran into Regent's Park. Trim stripped the wallet of cash, twelve quid, and said it was all his, danger money. Then he got me to wipe the wallet clean of his fingerprints and chuck it in the undergrowth.

'The park?' Phil was going. 'What park?'

'Oh, any old park. Or litterbin. Whatever.'

'What about your credit cards?'

'They've gone too.'

'Did you report them stolen? You know, to the company?'

'Oh yeah,' I breezed. 'I spoke to this woman on night duty at American Express. Name of Gayle. She was cool. I gave her all the details and she said how the new one was in the post.'

'Good to hear you can still get a live human.'

'Yeah.'

'But what about your mum?'

'My mum?'

'What's wrong with her?'

'She was in Wales on this surfing holiday, see.'

'Surfing?'

'She's a real sporty type. And this mega wave comes and turns the surfboard over and she bangs her head. On a rock.'

'Is she concussed?'

'She hardly knows where she is.'

'Sounds serious. What part of Wales is this?'

'Fishguard,' I said.

'Fishguard? Didn't know they do surfing round there.'

'Sure they do.'

'Well, I wish I could take you all the way. But when I pull into the yard in Carmarthen, I can probably get you a lift with another of our trucks, if you like. Some of the fellows go that way for the ferries.'

'The ferries? To Ireland?'

'Yeah.'

'That would be *great*.' Was I in luck. Fishguard? The ferries? Ireland? I couldn't believe the rest of the journey had landed in my lap. 'Ta 'n' all.'

Phil nodded. I went back to watching the white dividers, grinning ear to ear.

'What's in your truck?' I asked after a bit. Miko said that the truckies pick you up because they're lonely on the road and you have to earn your way by entertaining them.

Phil smiled like he was posing for a camera shot. 'Cheese,' he said. My stomach rumbled. I love cheese. 'Six thousand kilos of hard cheese. And you know what? I don't even eat it. You're with the one and only vegan truck driver in the whole of bloody Britain.'

There wasn't much to say to that. Phil sighed, like being a vegan was a tragedy, and got lost in his own sad vegan dream, with his face glued to the road, and the miles got eaten up quiet, with the radio rambling. If I was a vegan I'd be sad too. We passed pubs and lay-bys and hedges. I looked at the road signs and tried to figure them out. There were loads shaped like lollipops, sometimes with three strips on them, sometimes two and sometimes one.

We hit another stretch of dual carriageway and the tyres rolled smooth.

A song came on the radio and Phil turned it up. 'My favourite tune,' he said. ' "Katie Cruel".' I was expecting some old bit of pop but instead it was this lady sounding like she was being strangled by a boa constrictor, singing words that didn't make sense:

*'If I was where I would be,
Then I would be where I am not . . .'*

My brain did a spin with all the Ws. The trees by the road quivered with leaves. They blew in the wind and went white. *'Through the woods I'm going . . .'* Then there was a tree in the middle of a meadow with no leaves. It was dead and bare and sad for itself. *'Through the boggy mire . . .'* Phil sang along with a reedy voice

149

and I wished for cotton wool, the combination of the lady with the strangled voice and Phil was that disastrous. '*Straight way down the road back home to my heart's desire . . .*'

A grin landed on my face at the two of them yowling like two homesick dogs.

Then the song ended and the countryside changed. A sign said WELCOME TO GLOUCESTERSHIRE. Phil turned the radio down. 'That's what I call a *real* song,' he said.

'Telling me,' I lied.

'Country stuff's my favourite. What's yours?'

'I'm more of a rocker.'

'A rocker?'

'Yeah. Drums. Electric stuff. Y'know.'

There were hills in the distance and I saw a church spire sticking up. Then we passed a sign saying STRAWBERRY STALL AHEAD. Soon after there was a van parked in a lay-by with a table covered in boxes of bright red fruit and my stomach made a groan and *wham!* I remembered it was my birthday again.

11 June. Holly with green leaves and prickles, but no berries.

Strawberries always remind me of my birthday. At the Home we used to put all our birthdays on the wall planner, Miko's too, so nobody's would be forgotten. If it was yours, you got to choose dessert and mine was always strawberries and cream. I was in charge of putting the candles on the cake in the shape of whoever's age it was and Miko always let on his age was twenty-three, every year.

I thought of telling Phil it was my birthday, but then he'd ask how old I was.

'May as well stop for some food,' Phil sighed.

'Sounds like you don't like eating much,' I said.

'Out here on the road, all I ever eat is beans on toast with tomatoes.'

'Can't you have chips if you're vegan?'

He shook his head. 'Nine times out of ten, they fry the sausages in the same oil.'

My stomach rumbled at the thought of a sausage.

We went through a tunnel of trees and the road dipped and then we pulled off at a sign that said SERVICES. There was a restaurant and a petrol station. Phil parked up in a special place for trucks. He opened up this small compartment near the gearstick and I saw pound coins and silver in there plus some notes, thrown in careless. He took a couple of notes.

'D'you want to come in or stay here?' he asked.

I twirled my hair.

'You hungry?'

'I could murder a sausage,' I admitted.

'You couldn't,' Phil said. He smiled and his whole face crinkled like sun breaking through. 'Sausage is dead already, remember?'

I smiled back. 'Guess it is.'

'But I'll buy you one if you like,' said Phil. 'Come on.'

So in we went, the vegan truckie and Solace the glamour girl, the strangest pair ever to come out of a lorry-load of cheese.

Twenty-seven

The Birthday Party

The place was full of big men with bulging bellies and tattoos, just like you imagine truckies. Phil was a blade of grass among them and his sandals looked weird with everyone else in trainers. People stared as I strolled by in my zip-up top with the mint and rose dress peeking beneath and the high heels tip-tapping the lino.

Phil ordered the food. He asked if I wanted an egg and I said how eggs and me didn't agree. I got a table near the back and Phil brought me over a plate with two sausages and two slices of toast. I bolted them like a dog and wished I could lick up the salty juice left on the plate. He'd also got me a cup of milky tea with steam coming off. I poured sugar in and drank it and a tingle went into my fingers and brain. It was the first cup of tea I'd ever had and it was good.

Phil was chasing his last baked bean around his plate and still had his black tea to drink when I finished. 'Thanks, Phil,' I said. 'That was great.'

Phil blew on his tea. 'Never seen a sausage disappear so fast.'

'What were the beans like?'

'Same as beans anywhere.'

'D'you get bored of eating beans?'

'Sometimes.'

'How long've you been a vegan, Phil?'

'Since last year.'

'What made you give up meat?'

'I gave up dairy then. Meat was before, when I was a kid.'

'Why?'

Phil looked down at the last bean. 'My dad brought me to this sheep market when we were on holiday. A place called Week St Mary. Every time they sold a pen of animals for slaughter they'd punch a hole in their ears the size of a coin.'

'No way.'

'Yeah. Blood trickled down their ears and necks and the sheep baaed like they were being tortured.' Phil got out a pouch of tobacco and started rolling a fag. 'It put me off.'

I stared. He didn't seem the type to smoke.

'As for becoming a vegan,' he said, 'I did it for my health.'

His roll-up was all skinny and limp and wonky. 'Want me to make you one?'

The truth is, I didn't fancy it. I hadn't smoked in ages on account of being skint. *Clip-clop* went Ray's garden shears in my head.

'Nah,' I said. 'Thanks, but I've given up.'

'Yeah?'

'Yeah. Like you and the cheese. For my health.'

Phil slapped his thigh like I'd cracked a good joke. The crinkle came back in his face and his brown eyes twinkled.

I leaned over. 'Hey, Phil. Can I tell you a secret?'

'If you want.'

'It's my birthday.'

'What? Today? Why didn't you say?'

'With Mam sick and my stuff nicked, I forgot.'

'How old are you?'

' 'S top secret.' I looked at my fingernails and realized I'd been chewing them. 'I'm older than I look,' I said.

'Let's have another tea to celebrate,' Phil said. 'My cigarette can wait.' He went back to the counter and came back with a slab of strawberry cake along with the tea.

'Aw, Phil. You didn't have to. That's my fave.'

'I asked for candles but they didn't have any.'

'I'll just pretend they're there,' I said. I shut my eyes and wished, and what I wished is secret because if you tell, it won't come true, then I opened them and blew out the pretend candles and Phil clapped like I'd blown them all out in one and chirped a loud 'Happy birthday', and suddenly all the truckies in the café were clapping, and were my cheeks on fire.

'D'you want some?' I asked, digging in the fork.

'Can't,' said Phil. 'I'm a vegan, remember?'

'Not even a strawberry off the top?'

'There's only three,' he answered, smiling. 'And they've all got your name on them.'

I munched away. It was sponge and jam and strawberries and cream and I don't know when a birthday cake tasted better.

Twenty-eight

The Scenic Route

Phil smoked his fag and we went back to the lorry. I saw a fat truckie in the next one down struggling to get into his cab.

'You're not like other truckies,' I said as we drove off.

'What makes you say that?'

'You remind me of someone. A friend. And he's no truckie.'

Phil headed back to the road. 'I'm only doing it temporary,' he said. 'I'm planning my next move.'

'Oh, yeah? What?'

'Dunno. It's just quivering on that horizon like a mirage.' He took a hand off the wheel and pointed to the faraway blue hills. 'I can nearly see it. Only not quite.'

I laughed. 'You even *sound* like Miko. Miko's always saying how the road's like a key to the mystery of life.'

'Miko? Who's he?'

'An old boyfriend. We're just friends these days.'

'He has a point.'

'Maybe.'

'What does *he* do for a living?'

'Miko? He's a key worker.'

'A key worker? Like he makes locks?'

'Nah. A key worker's someone who works for social services.' I nearly said 'in a children's home' but I stopped myself just in time.

'Social services? Like a social worker?'

'Yeah. Before that he was a punk rocker.'

Phil shook his head. 'Never did get the hang of that. I'm strictly a country man.'

That was sad, very, so I said nothing.

'And you're a rocker, you say?' Phil asked after a bit.

'Yeah. Storm Alert's my fave. And TNT, some.'

'Never heard of those folk.' His lips drooped a little.

Then he turned up the radio. It was playing easy-listening tunes that made the sausages in my belly shrivel up. We passed a lay-by with three caravans and trailers and a dog – thin, like a greyhound, sniffing around some gas bottles – and a boy bashing nettles back with a stick.

'Travellers,' said Phil.

'Travellers?'

'Yeah, you know. Gypsy folk.'

I turned to get another look. Gypsies are people I like. Nobody else wants them, just like care-babes. I thought to myself if I get in trouble on this journey, I'll turn round and head back to them and join them and they'll give me a bed and a good-luck charm, and by the time the summer's over I'll be brown and dusty like them and people will queue up to have me tell their fortunes, on account of Solace having developed second sight.

'Here today, gone tomorrow,' Phil sighed. 'Maybe that's my next move. Take to a trailer.'

'Funny. *I* was thinking just that.'

'Maybe we're both wanderers, you and I,' said Phil.

'Yeah. And Miko. He's a wanderer too.'

Then Phil slowed coming up to a junction. It said GLOUCESTER A436 left, CHELTENHAM A40 right. And that's when it happened. He turned left, not right, clean off the road to Wales. Maybe he was a mass murderer after all, taking me to his lair, and I'd end up with my inside bits in polythene bags.

'Where we going?' I squeaked as we turned, clinging onto the wig.

'Huh? Oh, the Gloucester bypass. Saves time. It's a short cut. And more scenic.'

I breathed again. 'Oh, right.' The lorry straightened. 'Scenic. Cool.'

Then we passed a sign saying HUNT COUNTRY, a second sign saying HUNT COUNTRY, then a third saying 59% SAY KEEP HUNTING.

'What's with the signs, Phil?'

'Hey?'

'The hunting signs? Who's hunting who?'

'Oh, those. It's about fox-hunting.'

'Fox-hunting? The hounds and horses 'n' all?'

'Yeah.'

'It's mean,' I said. I thought of the stuffed otter in the museum in Oxford. 'It's cruel.'

'Yeah. I'm with the foxes,' said Phil. 'Which means I'm on the losing side. They'll still get hunted, whatever the law says. But hell, look at that view.' He pointed to the mountains pricking the clouds, a big chunk of country. 'Beautiful, huh? Soon we'll be in Wales, the land of singing and hills.'

Wales. Singing. Hills. I smoothed down my feather fringe in the side mirror and smiled. I counted the sheep in the next field: fifteen, the same as a certain birthday girl's age.

And that's when Fiona's face flashed through my head, and how the last thing she said to me before I left had been how there was a certain something she had to do for a certain somebody and that was why she'd be home late. I hadn't paid attention but now I realized: maybe she meant me and maybe the something was to do with my birthday.

But knowing Fiona she'd probably only intended fetching a carrot cake.

I bit my lip and stared out the window.

Warehouses flashed white. Then across a green field I saw a grand old tower. It had a top with four shining points, like a birthday cake with four candles.

'Gloucester Cathedral,' said Phil. He whistled through his teeth. 'Passed it so many times and never been up close.'

'Looks just fine from here,' I said. 'Up close,

maybe it's a let-down. Like some people – better the less you know them.'

'Sounds like someone's been giving you trouble.'

'Yeah, too right.'

'A boyfriend?'

'Not mine, my mam's.'

'*She's* got boyfriend trouble?'

'Big time.' There was a pause. 'See, Phil, that yarn I spun. About Mam and the surfing and the rock and knocking her head 'n' all. Wasn't really like that.'

'No?'

'She's got concussion all right. And some. This fella of hers punched her face and now she's two golf balls for eyes.'

'I'm sorry.'

'Yeah. She might as well put her head in a gas oven as hang out with that Denny-boy. He's a nightmare man.'

My eyes watered and Phil had to pass me a tissue. The only problem was I was crying years too late.

'We'll get you down there,' Phil said. 'D'you want to phone her?' He reached into his pocket and passed his mobile over. 'I should have offered earlier.'

My mind froze. I nearly said it was OK, I had my own phone, then I remembered mine was supposed to have been stolen, so I took Phil's and muttered a thank-you. I punched in a series of numbers that was nearly Fiona's but instead of the last digit I hit the # sign.

'Mam?' I said. ' 'S that you?'

All I could hear on the end was the whirl of

satellite dishes in outer space. Phil hummed softly to show he wasn't intruding, but how could he not hear every word when I was sitting right next to him?

'I'm on my way, Mam. Friend's giving me a lift . . . What? . . . I'll be with you this evening, Mam. Don't you worry. How's the head? . . . Where's Denny, so? . . . What? You *dumped* him? Like, you mean, for *good*? . . . Hey, that's great, Mam. *Great*. We'll go celebrate when you're . . . Yeah. You and me. Champagne. Girls' night out . . . What? . . . Telling me . . . Ta-ra-la, Mam.'

I made as if to hang up and handed him back the phone.

'Better?' said Phil.

'She's dumped him. Finally.'

'That's good news, then?'

'Sure is.'

We drove in silence and Phil turned the radio up. It was country-and-western disaster time but I didn't care any more. We got back on the A40 and then Phil said did I want to try another scenic route through the Forest of Dean? And I said yes, because the name alone sounded so scenic. Soon we were going up a windy road, past a sign that said:

LITTLE LONDON

PARISH OF LONG HOPE

which cracked me up. It didn't look like London, not even a small London, and if hope grew long here, that wasn't London either. Instead of tower blocks there were cream cottages and round hills, a blue sky with frilly white clouds, clumps of trees. There were road signs for deer. Any minute a magic white stag would bound across your path and make your wish come true. *Sweet dreams are made of this.* I smiled. We climbed up a steep hill, then over a low-slung wall came a view to die for. Treetops and houses like dots, and below that, a great river curling round like it had lost its way.

'Look,' Phil said. 'The Severn.'

My heart was in my mouth. I'd never seen anything so beautiful.

If I lived here, I thought, in one of those houses with storybook windows, would life be like a storybook too? Would it?

Twenty-nine

Down in Devon

Maybe the beauty made me tired. Yawns came up my throat like armies on the march and soon my head was rolling with the road and I was dreaming.

Miko was walking over the hill with a backpack, thumbing. When he saw me behind him on the road, he turned and called. I couldn't hear at first, then the wind brought the words of his crazy song over. '*Hurry, hurry, Holly Hogan,*' he sang. '*Before the road disappears . . .*' I ran to catch him up and fell, and I whirled down to earth like a meteorite and landed on the beach in Devon where Miko took us camping that last summer.

Grace was lying on the sand, with her lime-green towel and gold bikini and her caramel-smooth skin. Her belly button was winking high, and she made me come and lie with her. I was sorting out her braids. We watched the clouds above, moving slow like giant-breath, and Grace said, 'If you watch long enough, you float off with them and join the angels. It's like going to heaven, Holly, without having to die first.'

And Miko had his guitar out, strumming a stretch of chords, and Trim was kicking up trouble down by the breakers.

'*One, two, three, four,*' Miko hollered. He was half singing, half bawling, and making up the words as he went along. '*You can go on down that road, Holly Hogan,*' he sang off-key. '*That bad old road that swallows up your heart. Hurry, hurry, Holly Hogan. Before the road disappears. Before you end up falling, falling . . .*'

'Nah, Miko. Not like that,' I begged.

'OK, let's make the road go up, shall we? *That good old road that's like an escalator straightway up to heaven . . .*' Grace and Trim were yowling, blocking their ears, and Miko's song was all muddled up with the country song of Phil's, but I was flying with the beat. *If I was where I would be then I would be where I am not . . .* Miko was waving at me from the hilltop, going, going, gone, clean out of my life. And was being in the truck with Phil a dream I was having down on that Devon beach, or was the Devon beach a dream I was having up in the truck with Phil? And the notes of the song soared upward, like a military jet . . .

Thirty

The News on the Radio

. . . which is what passed over us, tearing the sky apart.

I woke with a jerk and yelped.

'Just a jet,' Phil said. 'Relax.'

'Bloody hell. Sounded like the end of the world.'

'It's the boys, back from Iraq.'

'Why do they have to fly so low?'

'Just their idea of fun, I suppose. Had a sleep?'

I stretched. 'Nah. Just daydreaming. About that friend I told you about. Miko.'

'The social worker?'

'Yeah, him.'

'Sounds like you still hold a torch for him.'

'Hey?'

'Wasn't he an old boyfriend?'

'Yeah. But he had to move away with his job. We petered out.'

Phil sighed. 'Same old story.'

'Too right. D'you have a girlfriend, Phil?'

'Me?'

'Yeah. You.'

'Not in ages. It's this job. You're never in one place long enough.' His hands rose off the steering wheel and fell back down. 'Maybe I'm better off single.'

'Know the feeling.' We passed these hedges that somebody'd shaved into giant hedgehogs, then a pond of lilies ringed by the kind of trees that hang down into the water.

'See them trees?' I said to Phil.

'The willows?'

'Yeah. Just thought up a joke.'

Phil grinned. 'Try me, birthday girl.'

'Why do willows weep?'

He sucked in his cheeks, then blew out. 'Dunno. Why?'

'They can't stand the sight of their own reflection. That's why.'

Phil hooted. 'Sounds like me the morning after the night before,' he said. 'Hey, look at that sign.'

I stared, but the letters didn't add up:

SIR FYNWY

'Who's Sir Funny?' I went.

Phil chortled. 'It's Welsh, for Monmouthshire. We're in Wales.'

Wales. You won't believe it but it was different, right away. We were running down a road with a brown mountain ahead. There were black and white cows in the field, all bunched up in one corner, sitting down. Then we passed a big tumble-down castle with a tower that wasn't ruined yet. In my head I put a woman on

166

top, like Mam maybe, in a long dress with floating sleeves and a cone on her head. Maybe she was waiting for Mr Right to rescue her or maybe she was waiting for me to come up the mountain road. Then a whole string of mountains loomed up. The radio made beeping noises and Phil turned up the volume.

'It's the news,' he said.

I didn't listen, but rooted in the lizard for my baby-doll lipstick. I needed touching up. The posh mogit voice droned in and out of my thoughts as I dabbed. *'Detectives are investigating the death of a baby in a fire in Leeds . . . The Archbishop of Canterbury has issued a statement expressing grave concern . . . In Pakistan, a bomb has exploded in the capital, killing fourteen . . .'* We went into a tunnel, with silver lights on one side and gold on the other. The radio crackled and I had to pause with the lipstick because I couldn't see in the wing mirror. We shot out of the tunnel '. . . *The Prime Minister has denied all knowledge of the memorandum . . . Police are searching for a fourteen-year-old girl who went missing from her south London home yesterday . . .'*

My heart forgot how to beat.

'. . . *She was last heard of in the Oxford area . . .'*

Thickhead, I thought. The call to the Gayle woman. They must have traced it.

'. . . *and do not suspect foul play but they are urging the girl to get in touch with her foster parents . . .'*

The road pounded on and I stared at the lipstick but didn't see it and I felt heat creeping up my cheeks.

Phil said nothing. I squinted over. His hands were on the wheel, same as ever, his eyes looking ahead.

Real slow, I moved the lipstick back up to my lips. I dabbed it on and dusted down the fringe.

'Pretty country,' I drawled over the mogit voice. 'Castles 'n' all.'

'What?'

'Wales. 'S pretty.'

'Sorry. I was miles off. That's the trouble with driving long distance. You get these times when you don't know where the last hour went.'

'Know the feeling. Like school.' Then I remembered I was Solace, all done with school. 'Mean, how school *was*,' I burbled. 'Used to blank out in science and technology. Only got two GCSEs.'

'I only got one.' Phil whistled out a long breath. 'And that was RE. Maybe I'll retake them one day.'

I looked at my bitten fingernails. 'So, Phil,' I said. 'When you drift off on the road, how come you don't crash?' The radio voice was on to the weather now, saying something about thunder and showers.

'Don't speak too soon.'

'Yeah. But how come?' I had to keep his mind off the news story somehow.

'Guess I go on automatic.' He glanced over. 'Do you drive?'

'Nah. Only people up a wall.'

Phil chuckled. 'D'you want to learn?'

'Yeah. I've got my provisional.'

'That so?'

'Yeah.'

'I love driving,' Phil said. He changed gear and

sped up. 'Only sometimes after hours of it the white lines hypnotize you. Then I put the radio on to keep my mind on the job.' He took his hands off the wheel for a split second. 'You hear all kinds of strange stories on that radio.'

Did he suspect me or not?

We crawled through a town called Abergavenny, stuck behind a pick-up truck. I stared at a takeaway place called Balti Bliss and at shops with odd things like washing machines, buckets and leather chairs spilling onto the street. I wondered if I should just hop out at the lights and run. But the chance to jump went when we got out of the town.

If he believed that girl in the report was me, I thought, *he'd have driven straight up to the police station.*

But even so, Phil kept glancing over at me like he was wondering something. Every time he did, that hot prickling crawled up my cheeks.

Houses clung to the slopes. I saw a big dead furry thing on the road with long hair, real thin, and flattened.

'Ugh!'

'That was a mink,' Phil said.

'A mink? As in mink coat?'

'Yeah. They're getting more common, apparently.'

What'm I going to do?

'The fur trade must be laughing,' Phil said.

The air got hot and sticky.

We went through another place, small and full of itself. It had rows of houses with flowerboxes on the sills, all pinks and mauves. I pictured old-people fingers sifting through them. Flowerboxes give me the mogit miseries. My stomach was churning.

The sky went dirty brown. The mountains got dark and close.

'Solace,' Phil said.

'Yeah?'

'I'm going to stop at the next petrol station, if that's OK.'

He's going to stop and ring the fuzz and turn me over.

'Sure thing.'

He pulled in a moment later and got down from the cab to fill up the tank. I sat there with my thoughts raging and my head thumping. I saw him get out his mobile phone.

Great. He'll look at the last call and figure it was a made-up number.

I opened the passenger door. 'Just off to the ladies,' I breezed. 'Won't be a sec.'

'I'll wait,' he said. 'Take care getting down.'

'Will do.' I made sure I had the lizard and climbed out.

'Solace?' Phil said.

'Yeah?'

'Are you in some kind of . . . ?' He frowned like he'd forgotten what he meant to say. 'Never mind. Nothing.'

I went in the toilet block and poured water over my face. There was no mirror.

Then I peeked through the crack in the door and guess what I saw. Phil on the mobile.

He's phoning the police. Gotta get out of here.

I froze. I could hear gravel crunching. Was he after me?

No, he was only going next door, to the gents.

Quick as lightning, I changed from the high heels back into my trainers.

I heard a toilet flush next door.

NOW, I thought. *RUN.*

I sped quiet as a kitten round the back of the toilets and along the road. I climbed over a gate and into a field and behind a bush. I could still see the petrol station and the truck, maybe fifty metres off.

Phil came out of the toilet building, hands in his pockets, looking around.

The world forgot how to spin.

He was waiting, leaned up against the wheel.

Maybe he was calling my name.

He walked round the toilets, knocked on the ladies' door.

Then he went into the shop.

Then he came out and waited some more.

He walked back to the truck.

He got his mobile out, looked at it and then looked up. For a moment it seemed like he was staring right at me, but then his gaze shifted and his shoulders slumped.

He got in the truck. But the engine didn't start.

Minutes passed. From far away came a distant rumble. Thunder.

Then the engine did start. The lorry pulled away. And Phil with it.

The world started moving again.

I sat down in the green field. Me and Solace and the lizard-skin bag.

The lizard flopped over like it was beat.

The girl inside me called Solace breathed out over the dandelions. *Close shave,* she whispered. She opened her palm and there were a couple of coins, stolen from Phil's stash. She couldn't help herself. She was a bad girl, that Solace.

But the real me didn't move. The Holly part was crushed, flat as the mink.

Thunder rumbled again.

Miko and Phil, same difference. Going, going, gone, story of my life.

Fishguard might as well be China.

I was in the middle of a field in Wales with a storm growling in the sky and the cops after me. And all I had to help was a thieving glamour girl who only existed inside my own cracked head.

Thirty-one

In the Black Mountains

Miko used to say you can meet God on the road.
Maybe he was right. I thought of Phil with his turned-
down lips and suffering eyes and sad music and him
buying me sausages when he was a vegan, not to
mention the birthday cake. And I thought of him
being sorry for my beaten-up mam in Wales and lend-
ing me his phone. I'd never really gone in for God
stuff. Souls floating up to heaven. People walking out
of tombs when they're supposed to be dead. Mam was
brought up Catholic on account of being Irish, but
she said churches were a waste of space and the
sooner they were all made into nice roomy flats
the better. But on that day of my fifteenth birthday,
11 June, I sat in that green field and thought maybe
God does exist a tiny bit. Maybe he kind of sits inside
people, looking out through their eyes. Maybe God
gets inside you and makes you do good things and you
don't even know he's there. He'd probably never
come near my sort. But people like Phil, with his
scenic routes and vegan dreams, he loves.

I looked at the money Solace had stolen from him and I felt like throwing it away. Then I thought I'd hang onto it and give it to the first homeless person I saw. Or put it in a church collection box. For now, I put it away in the lizard, in the secret pocket where Mam's amber ring and my SIM card were stashed.

There was only one chink of blue left in the sky and that was shrinking. I got up and went back to the petrol station. I went straight to the toilets and brushed my real hair. I put the wig back on and brushed that too. Then I went out and looked up at the ugly dirty cloud hunched up over the dark mountains. The air pressed up hard and yellow.

. . . *They are urging the girl to get in touch with her foster parents* . . . Fiona and Ray. I'd tucked them away into the back of my head, but now they were back times two. I could see Fiona looking at me that first time in my bedroom in Templeton House like I was the last whale, and Ray looking up at me from the garden below, smiling. *Clip-clop* went the shears, and the cloud-letters of my name floated across the sky.

They hadn't believed the story about me going off to Tenerife. Come to think of it, I didn't even have a passport.

One call, I thought, and it's over. They'll know I'm alive so they're off the hook, but they'll never want me back. Who could blame them? If I were Fiona and Ray, I wouldn't want me back either.

I got the mobile and SIM card out of the lizard and put them back together to see if they'd left me any more messages. But when I tried to turn it on, it died.

174

There was no charge left. But why would there have been any more messages anyway? They'd probably washed their hands of me.

The mountains darkened and there was nobody in sight. I popped into the petrol station, and with my own last bit of change I bought a Red Bull from the mogit woman behind the counter. Trim used to drink three Red Bulls straight off and then no one could stop him – not Miko, not anybody – he'd just roar and flare up and it was like you had to call in the vet to tranquillize him with a stun gun. I needed some of that, fast.

I sat on a wall and guzzled the drink. *Shake a leg*, I told myself. *Get back on the road before Phil phones the police and they hunt you down here like a fox.*

Then flickering started in the sky. I tramped down the road, thumbing as I went, but nothing much went by and nobody stopped.

The rain started. I turned off a side road, thinking the police were less likely to find me there, and sheltered under a big tree. I took off the wig and folded it safe away at the bottom of the lizard to keep it dry. There was a flash, then, a few seconds later, a thunderclap. I remembered the tree in *Jane Eyre*. Lightning splits it in two and Mrs Atkins says it's because Mr Rochester proposed to her under it when he shouldn't have, so Fate is angry because he has the wife in the attic. I reckoned Fate was angry with me too, for stealing the money off Phil. I moved down the road, looking for better shelter.

A pigeon flapped out of a hedge, scared crazy,

nearly stopping my heart. Then a loud clap exploded just across the next field. My insides and outsides swapped places. My life was one long list of wickedness. God had probably decided to murder me with a thunderbolt. I'd end up jellified in my shoes, a smoking mound of ashes. And it would serve me right.

I ran on down the narrow lane. Rain fell in heavy blotches, then started pelting so it hurt my skin.

I got to a strange bridge, made of stone with turreted walls, and under it a small river chasing.

I saw a flash and right after that a clap tore up the sky worse than that army jet. I screamed and cowered against the bridge wall.

'*Spare me, Jesus,*' I cried.

The lizard was sodden and soon everything in it would be drenched, including the wig.

I climbed over the wall and down the bank and got down under the bridge. The water was coming up around my trainers, but I didn't care.

Then I remembered. Mam. She'd been frightened of storms too. She'd drape blankets over mirrors to keep the lightning reflection from killing you. She'd draw the curtains. She'd take the phone off the hook. She'd pull all the plugs from the sockets. Then she'd lie on the tiger-skin sofa, moaning, 'Why do we have to live at the top of this bloody tower block, Holl? Why?'

The water was white and swirling. I huddled hard against the stone of the bridge. The storm rumbled and crashed, sometimes near, sometimes far. I got out the amber ring of Mammy's from the secret zip pocket in the lizard. There were no robbers anywhere to chop

off my finger so it was OK to put it on. *It'll keep me safe.*
It will. I put it on my middle finger and closed my eyes.
You could still see the lightning flash, even behind
your eyelids, so I opened them again and stared at the
tiny insect stuck in the middle of the amber. It had
been trapped there for hundreds of thousands of
years, Miko told me, the time I'd showed it to him.
He'd said how amber was made from the goo of pine
trees, only it was called resin and it had set hard long
ago, before there were people even. The dark speck
might be an ancient mosquito, Miko said. Or a fly.
I stared at it. Caught. For ever.
Mammy. Where are you?
Between the next crash and the next strike my
mind went white and clear and still.
And in the silence, she came to me.

'Holl.' Mam's voice calling, high and strong.
It's the sky house again with the glass, the balcony,
the light. I'm walking down the hall and there she is,
in the kitchen, fixing tea. Her face is covered over with
a see-through scarf. Like an eastern bride, her eyes
glitter through the material. Is she smiling? I can't see.
No, she's cross. She slams the knife drawer, opens a
can of baked beans. 'Go down to the corner shop,
Holl. Get the bloody fish fingers. I can't go. Not looking like this.'
The picture's burned out of my brain by another
lightning fork. Mammy's vanished. Instead there's a
knocking on the door and whoever it is won't go away.
So I open it and a woman from the Council's at the

177

door with a briefcase and she's smiling, looking down at me. I stare at the bracelet she has on, coloured discs, clacking against each other.

'Holly. Is your mother in?'

'No, miss.'

'Is her boyfriend there?'

'No, miss.'

'You're on your own?'

'Yes, miss.'

'Is your mum just down at the shop?'

'See that on your arm, miss?' I reach out and touch the bracelet.

'Do you like it, Holly?'

'Yes. 'S pretty.'

She takes it off and hands it to me. I make it click-clack and smile at the colours. 'Reminds me,' I said.

'What of, Holly?'

'Of Mam's drink.'

'Your mum's drink?'

'Not the colours. The noise. The noise of the ice.'

Then the lightning flashes again and Mam's taking off the amber ring, feeding it off her hand bit by bit, handing it to me, and her face is white and her hand is shaking. 'Look after it, Holl. Keep it safe. They'd chop your finger off for a ring like that.'

Look after . . . Look after . . .

A last grumble of thunder sounded away in the hills. The water swirled louder and the voices faded. Rain still spat down but the storm had rolled off, fast as it had come. I staggered out from under the bridge, straightening up. I looked at the ring, glowing on my hand. I stroked it, as if I could bring the tiny trapped insect back to life.

Oh, Mam. Don't go.

I looked around at the river and the banks, the bridge, the trees moving in the wind and the mountains. All the colours had gone grey in the strange storm-light. Then the clouds shifted, the sun slanted through, the greens and browns came back and the birds started up again. I fetched the wig out of the lizard, brushed through it and put it on.

I breathed. *There. There now.*

I wiped my eyes and smoothed down the dress. I shivered. I'd got chilled standing in the wet. I got the trousers out and put them on under the dress. Dresses over trousers were old, but down here in Wales maybe they were still reckoned cool, who knew.

Solace gave me a pep talk. *Holl. If you survived that storm, you can survive anything, girl. You're unstoppable. Telling you.*

My trainers squelched as I climbed back up to the road. I took them off and tied the laces together and dangled them from the lizard's strap. Then I put the sandals on. They hurt, but they were dry.

I made my slow way back up the side road to the A40. No storm would finish me off. No policeman would recognize me. I was a blonde, all grown up, not a brunette, aged fifteen. I'd thumb my next lift and hit the Irish ferries and I'd be free. *Mammy,* I thought, *stay right where you are. I'm getting closer with every step.*

Thirty-two

The Truck of Pigs

The road shone and the light was warm and strong after the storm. I stood at the top of a good clean stretch, near a gate that led into an enormous field of sheep. If you'd tried to count them, you wouldn't have fallen asleep, you'd have died of old age. I put my thumb out again, the amber glinting on my hand.

Nothing stopped. Cars and trucks passed, loud and fast. When they'd gone, you could hear the sheep baaing and wind tickling the trees.

I tried the dandelion trick again. Still nothing. Maybe I was the only person hitching in the whole of Britain, and maybe Phil was the only person crazy enough to stop.

After a long gap I glimpsed a car coming more slowly and I stuck out the thumb again. The vehicle was white and blue. I yawned. It rounded a corner and reappeared, getting closer.

That's when I realized. A police car.

Thickhead! I dropped the hand and turned, head

down, towards the gate and stared at the sheep. I wagged my finger like I was counting them.

Had they seen me? Were they looking for me?

Had Phil called the police after I'd done the runner?

I was sure the car was slowing, about to stop.

I kept counting like my life depended on it. In my head, they were taking me in and driving me to a cell and then they'd all come – Rachel, the police, Fiona and Ray, the psychiatrists – and they'd talk about me like I wasn't there. *Holly has chaotic high support needs*, I heard them say, shaking their heads, just as I overheard a social worker say once.

Chaotic. High. That was me all right.

But the police car quickened after it took the bend. It vanished up the road, leaving me behind. I breathed again. The wind played in the wig. The sheep baaed and I baaed back. One of them stared at me and I swear it was the spit of Trim. It had narrow eyes and a long snout and it looked like it would chew up the whole world and spit it right out. I laughed my head off by that gate and had to rub my side on account of the stitch I gave myself. If Grace had been there she'd have hee-hawed too.

Then I went back up to my spot on the bend.

A bone-shaker of a cattle truck rolled up. It was the kind with a cabin in the front and an open pen at the back, where they cram in the cows. But I couldn't see in because it was more wooden bits than gaps. I imagined it full of beasts heading for the chop. Soon they'd be swinging on hooks in a butcher's. I put my thumb out halfway, thinking of Phil being vegan, then my arm dropped to my side. But the truck still stopped.

I didn't move. A man opened the door and leaned out. He had a plump, round face and curly dark hair on the back half of his head. He was Addams Family meets Jack the Ripper, grinning ear to ear.

'Want a lift, love?' he said.

'Um,' I grunted.

'Where to?'

'Where're *you* going?'

'Lampeter.'

'No good,' I said. I rolled my wrist like I was queen of the land. 'I'm going to Fishguard.'

'I can get you past Llandovery,' he said.

I remembered Llandovery from the map, only he said it different, Clan-dove-ry. 'You mean Lando-very?'

He slapped his thigh. 'That's priceless. Like calling that dandelion in your ear a dan-*day*-leon.'

He screeched with laughter. I had to smile. I took the dandelion from behind my ear and tossed it aside.

'You coming or not?' said the man.

'What's in the back?' I could hear things moving and breathing and see shadowy shapes through the slits.

'Pigs.'

'Pigs?' My nose wrinkled. I remembered Phil and his story about the sheep having their ears punched before they were slaughtered. I stepped forward and peered between the slats and made out some pale bristles and dark patches. Then I heard snuffling and pawing.

'Don't you like pigs?' he said.

'I like pigs fine,' I said.

'Then what are you waiting for? They don't bite. Hop in.'

My brain seesawed. I thought of the police car and how I needed to get out of sight. On the other hand, this guy didn't make me feel safe the way Phil had. I stared hard at his eyes and the lines around them and thought, *He's just your average truckie, Holl. No axe murderer.*

'OK,' I said. I climbed into the cab and put the seatbelt on. I wasn't as high up as I'd been in Phil's lorry, and it was tattier and smelled of sweat and old fags. But when we took to the road, the white dividers batted by again like old friends. The truck rattled as if every last one of those pigs was tap-dancing.

'What's your name?' the man said. 'Mine's Kirk.'

I'd just spotted a plastic lozenge, dangling from the rear-view mirror. Inside was a picture of a woman, top half. She was blonde, blue-eyed and starkers. My stomach flip-flopped.

'Don't you have one?'

'Hey?'

'A name.'

'Oh. Yeah,' I said. 'Solace.'

Kirk cocked his head like a confused dog. 'Solace?'

'Yeah.'

He chuckled. 'Some name that. Exotic.'

He's probably harmless, I told myself. Lots of men like pictures like that. Remember that magazine Trim had? That was way ruder. And Trim was normal, wasn't he? Then I thought that calling Trim normal was like calling Hitler a saint. OK, Trim Trouble wasn't exactly normal. But I could handle him, right?

'You're very serious,' Kirk said. 'You look like the Inland Revenue's after you.'

'Huh?'

'The taxman.'

'Oh. Ha ha. No, he's not.'

'He's after me,' Kirk said. 'Haven't filed in five years. D'you want the radio on?'

'Nah,' I said. I didn't want any more news bulletins. 'Say, Kirk?'

'Yeah?'

'What's with the pigs?'

'Eh?'

'I mean, are they *your* pigs?'

'Nah. I'm just driving them.'

'So *where* are you driving them?'

'Like I said. Lampeter.'

'Yeah, but when they get there, what *then*?'

'I get it.' Kirk thumped the wheel and laughed. 'You're one of those animal rights people.'

'Just curious. I mean, are they for the chop or what?'

'This batch is heading to a pig farm,' he said. 'They're for breeding purposes, far as I know.'

'Breeding?'

'Yep. You can stop worrying, darlin'. By tonight they'll be rolling in clover. They'll be wallowing in mud. They'll be chomping the acorns.'

184

'Hey, Kirk. That's great.' I decided he was maybe better than he looked. I didn't care about the naked woman in the lozenge any more. I just thought about those pigs and how they were safe and how I was safe even if the truck was a bone-shaker, because nobody, not anybody, knew where I was. We drove on in silence, slicing through the puddles left by the storm. The mountains got bigger and mistier. They wavered like blue ghosts.

We passed an old stone pub lit all over with Christmas lights, although it was June and broad daylight. I remember Miko saying once that poor people put up the Christmas lights early because they're desperate for hope, while rich people put them up late, just before Christmas, because they have plenty enough hope already. I'd never seen lights in June before. The folks in that pub must be flat-out desperate, I thought.

We bypassed Brecon and I sat with my hand draped over the lizard, stroking my mam's amber.

'That's a pretty ring,' Kirk said, glancing over.

They'd chop your finger off for a ring like that. 'It's junk,' I breezed. 'Got it out of a Christmas cracker.'

'That was some lucky cracker,' Kirk said. 'All I ever get is God-awful jokes.'

'Know the feeling.'

'D'you want to hear the worst joke ever?'

'Try me,' I said.

'What lives under the sea and murders mermaids?'

'Dunno.'

'Go on. Have a guess.'

185

'A shark?'

'Nope.'

'A whale?'

'Jack the Kipper.' He screamed like it was the best thing he'd ever heard, and coming from a Jack the Ripper look-alike, maybe it was.

'That *is* bad,' I laughed. Some jokes are like that. A bit like my one about the willows. So bad they're good. It reminded me of this strange boy in my class at school, Max. He was so not funny, he was funny. He was in a class of his own. Max the Chap, we called him, on account of his BBC radio voice. He was a mega-geek who came top at maths and dressed like he was a mogit from fifty years ago. And d'you know what his hobby was? Bell-ringing. I ask you. *Bell-ringing?* I mean, it's so uncool, it's cool. I said to Karuna, maybe we should all go along with old Max and ring a few bells, ding-a-ling. She thought I was joking and laughed at me, but I thought me and Max and Karuna making some giant bells ring out over all south London would be cool.

The mountains got smaller. The road twisted and the cattle truck with it.

'Those pigs must be flying,' I said as we went over a bad bump. The white dividing line was unbroken, and painted on the tarmac every so often was

SLOW

ARAF

I stared and wondered what ARAF was. Maybe the

186

letters stood for something. Maybe 'All Roads Are Fatal'. I heard Miko wailing in his worst punk voice, '*falling . . . falling . . .*' Then I got it. We were in Wales, right? So ARAF was Welsh for 'slow'.

Then there was a sign saying LLANDOVERY 1 MILE.

Fishguard was getting closer every bend.

We drove straight through the centre of the town and over a train crossing, then out of the town and down a deep valley with rock-grey sides and plants growing out of it.

We came to a lay-by and Kirk pulled in. It felt like I'd only just got in and the ride was over already.

'The turn-off to Lampeter's coming up,' said Kirk. 'You might as well hop out here. Unless . . .' He shrugged his shoulders and grinned.

'Unless what?'

'Unless you fancy riding on with me and going out for dinner, maybe.'

A date with a guy with a hairline halfway back on his head and a loony sense of humour? The blonde in the lozenge swayed and I grabbed the lizard tight.

'Thanks 'n' all, Kirk.' The pigs in the back were scuffling like they wanted out. 'That's a real nice offer – only, see, I've got to meet my boyfriend.'

'Your boyfriend?'

'Yeah. We're taking the night boat to Ireland. We're starting over. A whole new life. He's going to train as a jockey and I'm going to train as a dancer.'

'A dancer?'

'Yeah. Strictly posh stuff. Ballet 'n' all.'

'Oh.' He looked disappointed. 'So you're moving over there permanent?'

'That's right. Me and Drew. We're Irish by birth, see.'

'Never.'

' 'S true.'

'Hair like that, I took you for a Swede.'

'Ha ha. Thanks for the lift.' I got the door open.

'Hey, Solace. Before you go. Don't I get one?'

'What?'

'Even a teeny-weensy one?' He pushed his lips out like there was a chance in a million I might be in business.

'Not today,' I called. 'The boyfriend would be mad jealous.' I leaped down and slammed the door and waved him on. The truck started up and Kirk shrugged a goodbye and his lips went down like he was broken-hearted, only I could tell he wasn't, he just thought it was funny. He let the brake out and winked and then his truck rattled back onto the road with the beasts in the back going bananas.

'Save it for the pigs, Kirk,' I called.

Thirty-three

154 Vehicles Later

The sun was going down behind the mountains. I'd no idea it'd got so late. I decided to count the traffic.

Ten cars passed. A lorry. Then fifteen more cars. Twenty-six. I thought of Jane Eyre on the high moors, having to bed down for the night in the long grass. She was Airhead Extraordinaire, that girl. She'd left her trunk on the carriage, left all her jewels behind, and now she had nothing. How stupid is that. If she'd gone off with Mr Rochester like he'd asked, she'd have been living it up on the Riviera, dripping with gems, wearing white gloves up to her elbows. But then, that whole story cracked me up. *I'd* have caught on to the wife in the attic at the first cackle. The author lady had something funny in *her* top storey, I reckoned. A white van. Number forty-seven. Here I was in the middle of Wales. I was walking along a green tunnel of road and the air was cool. No way was I going to lie down in a field tonight. I stroked the amber ring. Or lose my jewels, thank you.

A car zoomed up the road like it was in a chase.

Number sixty-three. I'd never heard an engine roar so loud. I put out the thumb but the rate it was going the driver would never see me, let alone stop. It overtook a car in front, taking the bend hard. Then I heard a *screech.*

My hands went over my ears. I imagined the car on its roof, spinning, like in the movies, and the petrol gushing out on the road, and the people inside mashed and all of it on fire. But I'd only heard a screech, not a crash.

A car came in the opposite direction, lights flashing, horn tooting. It must have been a near miss.

I grinned. Trim would have died to be in a car like that. I imagined him shooting up the motorways, Grace at his side, telling him to hug the white line smooth and strong.

But the smile went from my face when I remembered the little Kavanagh brat with his toy cars. I didn't like the Kavanaghs because they always sided with the kid, their pride and joy. I was the charity girl, a bit like Jane Eyre with her awful cousins. Anyway, this kid had a whole fleet of cars that he raced round the kitchen table. I remembered him zooming a green car off the edge so it clattered onto the floor. He stamped on it and went, 'You were in that, Holly Hogan. Now you're dead.' He had this scream when he didn't get his way that pierced your brain. If I'd screamed like that, I'd have been spanked, but *he* never was.

My time at the Kavanaghs' went on I don't know how long. Then this one day I woke up and found Mam's picture, which I kept propped up by my bedside, all torn to pieces on the bedspread. And I screamed, big time, louder even than that boy. There was a bit with her bare foot and ankle in the sand, torn. Then half her arm, keeping a floppy hat on against the wind. Her middle was ripped so you could see half of her green bikini. Her face was shredded so small you couldn't see anything, no lips, no eyes, nothing. I howled fit to bring the roof down. Mrs Kavanagh came in and shouted at me. I pointed at the torn picture and said how the kid had done it because he hated me. She snorted and said how I must have done it myself, because her boy would never do that, would he? I drummed my feet on the mattress. Then the bedside lamp went flying through the window. And that was the end of the placement.

A hundred cars and lorries, dead on, and no lift.

Grace had had ten placements, which made her Placement Princess in Templeton House. But none had gone right. Trim hadn't had any. You'd have to be mad-crazy to take him on. As for me, the one with Fiona and Ray was definitely the last. *Your name's made out of cloud, Holly.* I squidged my eyes tight, but I kept hearing Ray's voice.

I thumbed and thumbed. A hundred and thirty and counting. These funny biting flies buzzed round my head. I waved my hands round and walked faster, but they just followed. It was enough to drive you crackers. To see me hopping and itching, you'd have thought I was crazy.

Nobody was going to pick me up acting like this.

A bus came by and I tried sticking my hand out, but it didn't stop.

I counted 153 cars and lorries, and one bus. Which makes 154 vehicles passing and no ride.

Hurry, hurry, Holly Hogan, the song went through my head. *Before the road disappears beneath your feet.*

At this rate I'd be sleeping in the long grass after all.

Thirty-four

The Boy on the Motorbike

Vehicle 155 was a whole other story. It didn't have four wheels, only two. A motorbike. It came round the corner so fast I only stuck my thumb out just in time. A miracle. It pulled in just ahead of me.

I hip-hopped up to it fast as I could in my high heels. It was like going up to an alien invader on account of you could see no face, just a black space helmet and black leathers.

'Hi,' I called.

There was no answer.

Maybe this alien didn't speak English.

When I got nearer, the alien pulled his head off. Joke. He pulled his helmet off. I half expected there to be no head inside, but it was just a boy with spotty cheeks. If I had acne that bad, I'd wear a helmet too, permanent.

'Do you want a ride?' he asked in a sing-song voice.

'Yeah, ta.'

'I'm only riding myself,' he said.

'Whatever.'

'Where you going?'

'Fishguard.'

'Fishguard, is it? That's far.'

'Got a boat to catch.'

'Can't take you all the way there.'

'Whatever.'

'Me and Andúril here' – he tapped his bike like it was a racehorse – 'we're just cruising.'

'Andúril?'

'The bike's name. Haven't you heard of Andúril?'

'Nah.' He waited and I could tell he wanted me to ask. 'So who's Andúril?'

'You mean, *what's* Andúril.'

'OK, *what's* Andúril?'

'It's Aragorn's sword, right?'

I blanked.

'Aragorn in *Lord of the Rings*, right?'

'Oh, yeah. The thingy with the orcs and elves.'

'*The blade that was broken has been remade*,' he crowed. He tapped the bike and revved it up.

I had to smile. 'Right,' I said. 'Remade.'

'D'you want to get on then? I'll take you to Llandeilo,' he said. 'Maybe you can get a bus from there.'

'Cheers.'

He opened a compartment in his bike and took another helmet out. 'Better put this on,' he said. 'It's the law.'

'Sure thing.' I put the helmet on over the wig. Then I hitched the lizard tight on my back and climbed up behind him, sitting astride. My heart was hammering.

'You can put your arms around my waist if you want,' he said.

I knew the type. He was one of the Less-than-Rare-Spotted-Non-Scorers, as Grace calls them. I kept my arms by my side, but soon as he started, I shrieked and grabbed him by the jacket.

I can't tell you much about the first part of the journey on account of my eyes were shut tight. I just smelled his leathers and felt the cold wind.

I might have died ten times on that bike. Every time he took a bend, you had to raise your knee in case it scraped the ground. I could tell he liked me clinging on. But if I didn't cling on I was dead. Then I opened my eyes. I let my cheek rest against his back and looked at the hedges flashing past. I saw whites and purples, creases in the tree trunks, and the road rushing past with pieces in the tarmac shining silver.

I made my spine stand straight. *Wake up, girl. This is a blast.* The green leaves shimmered overhead and it felt like we were going a hundred miles an hour.

'Go faster,' I screamed to the boy.

I don't know if he heard me but we sped straight as a bullet, ahead to the blood-orange sun that floated on the hill like an overblown balloon. The motorbike jumped in the air like a hiccup. Then a lorry screeched coming round a corner, and I thought we were dead. I clung on and shut my eyes and I could feel the boy laughing.

Then we hit the town. Houses, pavements, signs. He slowed. He braked so hard coming up to traffic lights, it was like being kicked. The lights turned. He sped forward like he was on a mission and my behind nearly slid off the back.

He stopped hard by a graveyard, and I thought that's where he was headed again very soon – only under the ground, not over.

I got off. My legs had turned to spaghetti.

'End of the ride,' he said. 'Llandeilo.'

'Yeah, ta.'

'You liked it?' he asked.

'Oh. Yeah. 'S great.'

'We weren't too tame for you?' He gave Andúril a pat.

'Nah.' I got the visor of the helmet up and struggled to get the thing over my ears. I could feel the wig riding up with it.

'D'you want a hand?' he said.

'Nah, I'm all right, ta. Say. What's with that strange bird on that tomb?'

He turned round to look and I got the helmet off quick. The wig came off too, so I thrust it back on and patted it down.

'What bird?' He was puzzled.

'The black one. An eagle or something.'

'Eagles aren't black.'

'A raven, then.'

'Can't see it.'

' 'S gone,' I said, fiddling with the wig's fringe. 'Never mind.'

He turned back to me, put his visor up and stared. 'Your hair's all wild,' he said.

'I'll straighten it later.'

'I like it the way it is,' he said.

I could tell he didn't want to go. I gave him my best smile. 'Ta for the ride.'

He cleared his throat. 'What's your name?'

'Solace,' I told him. 'I'm the one and only Solace in the whole wide world.'

'Neat name.' He was looking into my eyes. I shrugged. He was bright red. 'Well, Solace, good luck catching the boat.'

'Oh, yeah. The boat. Ta.'

'Fare thee well, Solace,' he said. He bowed, real formal, like I was queen of the elves. Then he put his visor down, raised his spaceship glove in the air.

I watched the mirrors and handlebars flash blood-orange in the setting sun as he zoomed away on his reforged sword that would be broken again in two shakes. I clucked my tongue and shook my head. 'Flat-out crazy,' I murmured. I realized I knew the bike's name, but not his. Shame. Apart from the spots, he'd been all right. Grace would have wrinkled her nose on account of the state of his skin, but he'd had nice dark eyes and his leathers smelled good. Now if *he'd* asked for a kiss, I might have obliged. You never know. I chuckled at the thought of him liking my hair and saying 'Fare thee well'. Not to mention that I wasn't lying on the highway like scrambled eggs.

Thirty-five

The Ghost Town

I looked about at the graveyard where he'd left me. There were tall trees and a strange crooked light coming through the clouds, the kind you get before a storm. And the wind was up. *Not more thunder,* I thought. *Please.* It was June and the day lasted long after the sun was gone. But the graves were black domes and crosses and I could hear the crows ha-ha-ing over the dead bodies. I sat down on a bench.

Then I remembered the money I'd taken from Phil, stashed in the lizard, and the promise I'd made myself to give it to a church on account of him having God inside him. I walked around the building until I found a door and tried the handle but it was locked.

I wriggled it back and forward but it didn't budge.

Somehow that locked door made my eyes fill up.

I pictured the benches and the smell of old stone and the quiet and how if another storm was coming I'd be safe inside, and what was I to do next?

It started spitting again.

I'd always liked rain, but now it was different.

Solace was a strictly sunshine girl, she couldn't get wet.

I wandered out of the graveyard and down a main street. It was long, with fancy pubs and hotels. I prowled down it, but it was empty. Then a black and white dog with neat, clicking paws came towards me. It had lonesome eyes and raindrops on its wavy fur. I held my hand out. It sniffed and licked and tried to jump me. It was shaggy and smelled of bonfire and I thought of Mam telling me about Irish dogs and how they're different from London dogs. London dogs trot around on leads with their heads in the air, like they're oh-so-elegant. Irish dogs take naps in the open doorways and wouldn't be seen dead on a lead, but when you drive up in a car they chase your wheels and bark as if you've got four hares spinning round instead of tyres.

'Hey, dog,' I called. 'Down, down.' I patted its head and scratched its chin and then the dog rolled over and showed its belly, which means it trusts you. And it had nipples, which meant it was a girl. I rubbed her belly and the rain got harder. 'What's your name, girl?' I asked her. 'Rosabel, maybe?' The dog suddenly sprang up like she'd heard an invisible whistle. She cocked her head and scampered off. I watched her go and sighed.

Story of my life.

The wig was getting sodden and I had no choice but to take it off. There was nobody about, so I put it safe away in the lizard and hobbled off down the street in my heels.

I passed a pub with its door wide open. It didn't

have much custom, just one tired old man. He was hunched over the bar, not talking, staring into his pint. His face was lined like crumpled paper. There was no sign of a barman. I nearly went in, then remembered that without the wig I was under age. Maybe it's a flat tomb for a bed after all, I thought. My feet hurt. A bus shelter loomed up so I stepped inside and changed back into my trainers. They were still damp, but they were better than the heels. I looked around. It was the kind of bus shelter where if you think there's a timetable, think again. As for a bench, forget it. There was a gob of chewing gum on the glass, that was all.

Maybe it was a bus shelter where no buses ever stopped.

Maybe the rain would never stop either.

Maybe I'd reached the end of the road.

Maybe I'd reached the end of the world.

I leaned against the glass and stared at the rain splattering the other side and time passed.

No buses, no cars, no people. Just crows cawing, and rain drizzling, and wind whistling ghost-like through the trees.

Thirty-six

The Getaway Car

I kicked the side of the bus shelter. Over the road, a curtain twitched. I felt like putting a brick through the window on account of curtain twitchers are the saddest mogits of all. I'll never grow up to be a curtain twitcher, I thought. I'll kill myself first.

But at least the curtain twitching meant there was life *somewhere* in this place. The ghost-town spell was broken. Then a woman, youngish, half mogit, came dashing towards me down the street with the rain clouds chasing her. Was I pleased to see her. She was definitely alive. The mogit bit of her wore a cardigan over an ugly blue dress, but the non-mogit bit was trotting in heels in the middle of the road, as if no cars ever drove on it, with a set of keys swinging from her fingers. She had a bag slung over a shoulder.

'Hey,' I called. 'Are there any buses in this place?'

I thought she was going to ignore me, but she paused and looked across to where I was.

'The last bus left an hour ago,' she panted in the same sing-song voice the boy had had. That was Wales

201

for you. It wasn't like Ireland, but getting closer. 'You're out of luck,' she said.

'Oh,' I said. 'Great.'

'Where are you going?' she asked. 'It's getting late.'

'I didn't know about the buses stopping so soon,' I told her. 'Mam will be furious.'

'Where are you going?'

I pointed down the road, the direction she'd been running in, and frowned like a baby does when it's trying to cry but has forgotten how. I wasn't *really* crying, you understand. I was just seeing if I could raise a lift.

'I'm driving to Carmarthen, if that's any use,' she said.

'Carmarthen?' That was where I'd have been hours ago if I'd stuck with Phil.

'It's where I work. Any good to you?'

'Sure is. That's where we live, Mam and I. Carmarthen.'

'Which bit?'

I blinked away the crocodile tears. 'Near the centre?' I squeaked.

'I work at the hospital.' She tapped her dress and I guessed she was a nurse. 'I'll drop you off by the bus station. Don't see how you'll get home otherwise. But hurry. I'm late.'

'Yeah, ta.' I pattered after her down the street to where her car was parked, a little thing that looked like if two people got in it would fall apart. She tossed some papers and a sweater to the back to clear the passenger seat and we climbed inside. It felt low to the ground after the lorries and boxed in after the motorbike, but it smelled of fresh flowers. It was the smell of her perfume – and the perfume was the same as Mam's. It was almost like Mam was in the car too, only invisible.

The nurse woman started the car and pulled out, doing her seatbelt up at the same time.

'So what were you doing in Llandeilo?' she said.

'Visiting,' I said. Then I added, 'My friend Holly. It's her birthday.'

'Couldn't her parents have dropped you back, this time of evening?'

'Their car's broken down. Else they would've.'

'Maybe you should've stayed over. A sleepover? Isn't that what you girls do these days?'

'Sometimes. But not school nights.' I spoke like I was an old hand but nobody'd ever invited me on a sleepover and it's not like I could have asked anyone over to Templeton House. I guess I could have tried asking Karuna over to the Aldridges' place, but Karuna's a) a rude-girl, b) a nutter, and c) Fiona would have fainted at the sight of her blood-orange nail polish.

'Do you like school, then?'

''S OK.'

'You're not from Wales, are you?'

'Nah. My mam's Irish. But we used to live in London.'

'London? What bit? I trained in London.'

'We used to live up by Harrods. In a flat. Mam used to take me in there to look at the things.'

'Lucky you. Can't even afford to *look* on a nurse's salary.'

'They've got good bargains,' I said. 'In the sales.' I patted the lizard. 'My mam bought me this in there,' I said. 'Cost a skin-diver.'

'A skin-diver?'

'Fiver. Cockney-rhyming-effin'-blindin'. You know.'

The woman laughed and threw the bag a glance. 'It's nice, that. A deal. My name's Sian, by the way. S-I-A-N.'

'Sian?' It sounded like 'sharn' and made me think of smooth green hills. ''S pretty.'

'People always think it's Irish, but it's Welsh. What's your name?'

'Solace.'

'Solace?' said Sian. 'That really is pretty. Where did it come from?'

'Mam called me that. She had this little boy, see. Denny-boy. But he died tragic. He was knocked down by a lorry, aged five. Then I came along right after and Mam said I was what was left when all else failed.'

Sian sighed. 'That's a sad story. Very.'

We passed these swampy-green fields, and the clouds bunched on one side and on the other the sky was dark-blue velvet. Sian put her foot down and the car bucked like a racehorse, the kind that barely makes it from the stalls. Then we passed one of those signs that have old-fashioned cameras drawn on them and Sian braked hard and the car burped and changed its tune.

'Whoa!' she exclaimed. 'Always forget those speed

cameras. I'm the world's most impatient nurse. My patients are lucky they don't end up with cardiac arrests, seeing me spin round with the drugs trolley.'

I laughed, thinking of the smooth white floors in the hospital and Sian whizzing round it, running over people's slippers.

Then we hit another sign:

CARMARTHEN
WALES'S OLDEST TOWN

'We've skirted the worst of that shower,' Sian said.

The place was white houses and grey roofs crawling up a hill. There was a grim tower in the middle that reminded me of the ones you could see from the sky house, only its windows were dingy and dark instead of silver.

'How long have you lived here?' Sian said.

'A year, nearly.'

'D'you like Carmarthen?' she said.

In that dim light you'd have to have been daft to like it. I could see car parks and estates and the dark tower hovered over it all like an evil spirit from a fantasy world of orcs and elves. But when someone's giving you a ride, you act polite.

'It's all right in the right light,' I said.

Sian laughed. 'First time I ever heard Carmarthen described like that,' she said. 'If you ask me, it's a dump-hole. Whatever the light.'

'That's what Mam says. She says it's worse than a Holy Day of Obligation.'

'What's a Holy Day of Obligation?'

'It's a Catholic thing. Irish. It's a day when if you don't go to church, you go to hell.'

'Sounds bad.'

'Yeah. Mam says that about all the things she doesn't like. Elevators. Thunder and lightning. London. And her old boyfriends.'

'I must tell my own fellow that next time he plays up.' Sian giggled and I joined in. And suddenly we couldn't stop laughing. It was like Mam was in the back seat with her flowery perfume and we were all in a getaway car, Solace and Sian and Mrs Bridget Hogan.

I could have driven all night and day in that car with Sian but soon we pulled up at the bus station.

'You know your way?' she called as I climbed out.

'Yeah, Sian. Ta.'

Sian smiled, then yawned. 'Tired before I start. Great.'

'You gotta work through the night?' I asked.

'Yes. Night duty pays better.'

'That's what Mam used say.'

'Oh?'

'She did night duty too.'

'Nursing, was it?'

'No. Dancing.'

Sian's eyes went impressed. 'Really?'

'She's retired now. From the stage.' I twisted the strap of the lizard. 'She just dances in the garden these days. Around the lawn. Under the washing line. When no one's looking.'

'Ballet or modern?'

'Modern mostly. Exotic.'

'Exotic? Like in a nightclub?'

'Yeah. But only posh nightclubs. Knightsbridge, mostly. That's why we lived near Harrods. Nothing seedy.'

'Sounds great. Do you dance too?'

'Nah.'

'Shame. You've got the figure for it.'

'D'you really think so?'

'Yeah. A dancer if ever I saw one. But you'd best get home, Solace. It's late.'

I said goodbye, closed the door and smiled. *You've got the figure for it.* I felt my slim-slam hips and thought of Grace saying I should lose ten pounds and how my neck was too thick, not like hers, which looked like somebody'd stretched it. Not to mention my miserable hair.

Sian drove off, waving. Her little car bucked as it drove down the street. I waved back. *So long, Sian.* It was like she heard, the way she hooted a reply.

The simplest lift of all time. I hadn't even had to hitch, and what can be safer than a ride with a nurse, even one that might run you over with her drugs trolley?

Thirty-seven

Carmarthen

Sian's car vanished and I pictured Mam in a green garden, neck and legs long, a shirt flapping on the washing line and her dancing with it like it was a partner.

'Mind out the way,' a bloke said, knocking into me as he hurried by. I looked at where I was. A dump-hole was right. I was in a dismal square with bus stops and cracked glass and stray people wandering around like the undead. I walked along, but Mam wouldn't leave my head. Her eyes were sad and she was stripping – not her clothes, just the amber ring. She was moving it up and down her finger, again and again, then holding it out to me.

I found a place to buy chips and curry sauce and bolted them down. It was Phil's money I used, or most of it. The change I stuffed in my skater-top pocket. I felt bad. Phil wasn't your usual truck driver, he was a vegan in whom God had taken up residence. But I'd have starved otherwise.

I got a drink from a dirty tap in the public toilet

and changed back into the heels. Bad move. I staggered down a hill with damp paving stones and nearly went flying. So I sat down on a wall near a car park and put the trainers on again. Was I sick of those high heels. Maybe it was how I'd stolen them from charity made them bite back. I kicked them away into the gutter.

The first streetlamp came on and made me look up. That's when I saw the police station, right opposite.

Bet there's a police report out now, with a full description.

I wondered if maybe going in there would be better than sitting on that wall in that wind in the dark in Carmarthen, with the undead wandering around.

Then I thought I needed a police cell like I needed a broken jaw.

No one was looking. I took out the wig and put it on so I could go back to being brave, unstoppable Solace. I gave it a good brush down and stroked the fringe tidy and walked back the way I'd come.

Then I found another phone box. I went in and arranged the lizard on the shelf and picked the receiver up and put it to my ear while people chased by, and I opened and shut my mouth like I was having an all-time hilarious phone-festival with my best mate. I talked and laughed up a storm even though there was nobody on the other end.

First I yattered away to Miko, then Grace, then Trim. Then Karuna. I even said 'Hi' to mad Max the bell-ringer. Then I thought I'd say a quick hello to Fiona.

'Hi there, Fee.'

Holly – is that you? (Fiona, frantic.)

'Yeah. Hi 'n' all. Been a while.'

Holly! Where've you been? We've been out of our minds.

'Dunno. Just cruising, having a ball. You know what it's like.'

Holly. Come on home. Please, Holly. We're missing you. Ray and me. Missing you, missing . . .

Yeah, in my dreams. I stared at the receiver. By now Fiona and Ray would have given up on me. Ray would have got his job up north and they'd be packing their bags. I shivered. I stroked the smooth fake skin of the lizard on the phone shelf and I remembered Fiona buying it that time in the market, down Tooting Broadway. It wasn't from Harrods, like I told Sian, and it wasn't from Mam. It was a gift from Fiona. I'd been trailing behind her as she pushed through the crowds on Tooting Broadway, shopping, and I'd stopped by the handbag stall, my favourite. I was doting on the bags shaped like animals – kangaroos, and cats, even a curled snake – and the ones with bright flowers sewn on and a lime-green one that made my hands itch. Fiona turned round and saw me looking. She smiled. She walked back towards me. The sun was on her face. She popped her sunglasses up onto her head.

'You always stop here, Holly,' she said. 'Every time.'

'Yeah.'

'You like that one?'

'Yeah.' I moved my hand from the lime-green to

210

feel a bag that was hairy like a coconut. 'Mam used to say you could tell a well-dressed lady by the bag on her arm,' I said.

'Really?' Fiona looked over her shoulder at the battered black backpack she used for shopping. 'That counts me out.'

Next I stroked a bag made from fake tiger skin.

'Maybe you prefer that one?' Fiona said.

It reminded me of how our sofa looked in the sky house and I nearly said yes. Then I remembered how Denny-boy used to loll on it, his lip plopping in his sleep.

'Nah. I like that one best.' I pointed up to where the lizard was hanging, dangling and catching the light. I'd had my eye on it all along. It was a class act: silver-green with back straps and three zips with leather pulls like forked tongues and the skin crinkled and cracked like a real lizard.

Fiona grinned. 'It's wild,' she said. 'Original.'

She reached and unhooked it and the stall lady said it was nine pounds, but we could have it for eight.

I knew Grace would have killed for that bag on account of she adored reptiles of all kinds and dreamed of having a pet snake draped round her neck. I got out my purse and looked to see how much I had, but Fiona put her hand over mine.

'Holly,' she said. 'My treat.'

'But my birthday's ages away.'

'We'll call it an un-birthday present then.' She handed over the money and the stall lady passed the bag to me and I took it and hitched it on my shoulder and put my purse inside it safe. The lizard slid into place like it belonged.

'It looks great,' Fiona said. 'Striking.'

It felt like Christmas on that busy street with the teeming pavements. I grabbed the strap and did up a zip. 'Ta, Fee,' I said. 'Ta a load.' Fee was what Ray called her. I'd never called her that before, it just came out.

Fiona's lips went in between her teeth and she looked away. Her hand skirted my arm, then dropped to her side. She smiled and stepped back into the passing crowd. 'Let's get on with the shopping, Holl,' she said. I walked behind her, stroking the lizard and thinking of all the different compartments and what I could put in them. I forgot to be angry that Fiona'd called me Holl. I was walking on air all down Tooting Broadway.

The phone receiver sat in my hand with no Fiona at the end of it. I slammed it down. The lizard was sprawled on the shelf, looking tired. The zip fasteners had frayed a little and the sheen had been dampened down some in the rain. Outside all the streetlamps had come on, and the crowds rushed past like time had speeded up. Fiona was going, going, gone. It wasn't Tooting out there, but Carmarthen, Wales's oldest town.

Thirty-eight

The Station Platform

I nearly went back to the police station then. I imagined myself going in and saying to the sergeant on the desk how I was a runaway and I had chaotic high support needs and could they take me in please and send me home. Only there'd be a case conference and everyone would say how I'd broken my promise not to run away again and I'd get twenty-eight days renewable, like Trim, and I'd rather have died.

It's for your own good, Holly. Everyone said that except Miko, who always used to be on my side, whatever. Miko raved on about how he was wild in his youth, worse than us lot. Once he spent a night in jail for being drunk. When the police made him take everything out of his pockets, he turned out twelve conkers that he'd collected after drinking a bottle of whisky. He said how he'd given up the booze five years ago just before his liver packed up, but he still had to go to meetings and promise to stay sober.

To get out of the secure unit I'd had to make promises too. Not to run away. Not to go hooking on the streets. I was so desperate to get out I'd have sworn to become a nun. I had to make my words real by writing them down. Then they let me out. And now, because I'd broken that promise, I could make ten promises and they'd never believe me again. I was finished.

I walked on into the crowd and past the pubs and the empty shops and under a clock with a face lit up cheerful. I wanted to smash it like I'd wanted to smash the windows on Mercutia Road the day I left. I saw a bottle in the gutter and picked it up.

Then the minute hand clicked to eleven o'clock. The clock whirred and started chiming. *Dong-dong.* Less loud than Big Ben, louder than Fiona and Ray's tick-tock-no-luck carriage clock. I smashed the bottle on the kerb instead and kicked the shards onto the road.

Just what are you so angry about, Holly? It was Miko's voice, so loud in my thoughts I nearly jumped.

Dunno, Miko, I replied in my head. *Different stuff.*

If you ask me, it's the same old thing, over and over, Holly, the same old story . . .

I went on down dark streets, walking in circles, and my anger turned scared and sad.

'S dark, I thought.

'S cold.

Gotta find somewhere to hole up.

Homeless people wrap themselves up in cardboard and curl up under bridges and pee against the walls like dogs. I didn't fancy it.

I thought of better places. I made a list in my head.

214

Churches
Cinemas
Sheds
Houses where the curtains aren't drawn, showing how the owners are on holiday

Churches get locked up at night, like the one I'd tried earlier. Cinemas chuck you out after the last show. Sheds are good but you have to break into them. Same goes for houses where the people are gone. Knowing my luck, I'd get caught breaking in by the people returning right at the wrong time.

Then I turned a corner and saw a sign for the train station.

The train station. That's it.

Miko had told me about sleeping rough in stations when he was on the road and cash-free, as he put it. He said how he'd snuggled into his sleeping bag on the concourse along with the homeless and raving weirdos, and how the trains left and arrived in the night and a woman kept calling out the stops, and nobody hassled him. *I washed and brushed up the next morning in the gents, Holly. I pretended it was the Ritz.*

I smiled, thinking of Miko shaving his chin in the grimy mirror, acting like he was out of the top drawer. I followed the sign and found the station. The ticket office was shut and nobody was around. You could just walk through to the platforms. I stood looking at the train timetables like a serious traveller planning my next move. That's how I found out about the late-night train. What I saw was:

215

For a minute I thought it was a midday train. Then I saw how it had to mean 47 minutes after midnight. Then I thought it must just be a Saturday or Sunday train. Then I thought maybe it was an old timetable and no train would really come at a time like that when I was the only one on the platform and there was no guard to check my ticket. Then I thought I didn't know what platform it would stop at. And 00.47 was ages away.

But inside my skin, I'd livened up something serious. *That train is your fate*, I told myself. *Fishguard is your birthday present.*

I crossed over and walked up along the other platform where I'd spotted an electronic sign. The amber message said the next train was the 00.47 to Fishguard Harbour. *Told you. A train with your name on it.* I sat on a cold bench and did my lips. I had one hour and thirty-nine minutes to wait. I put Storm Alert on and hugged myself and stamped my feet while Drew sang in my ear: 'Somebody's Working Late'. I'd never caught on to this track before, but now I did. I played it three times over. Then I thought of Ray, in his office, working late into the night, north of the river. He was hunched over his desk with the reading lamp on and Fiona was chafing at home, waiting. I skipped to the next track.

The cold got into my bones. I took out the earphones. My nose was dripping. Part of me was on that bench, and part of me was back down the road I came. I had to keep pinching myself so I didn't drop off the seat and then I'd look down the dark track and think, *I'm gonna be here for ev-er. I'm gonna be here for ev-er. For ev-er.*

I could get down and lie on that track on those things they call sleepers, I thought. And I could sleep *on the sleepers. Sleeping slipping on the sleepers sleeeeeepslipslip*—

I started in a fright and pinched myself. I'd been looking down on the track, almost falling onto it. The train would've come and gone over me and I'd have been scrambled eggs, only I wouldn't have known it. I wouldn't have known anything ever again.

I kept pacing the platform.

Then a rumble came in the distance. At first I thought it was thunder. Then I thought of the old trains in movies, how steam rises around the wheels. I listened. The noise stopped and I thought I'd imagined it.

No. There it is again.

A light went from red to green. Electricity hissed down the rails. I peered into the dark and saw lozenges of light coming round a bend, getting closer.

It won't stop, I thought.

A carriage whizzed past. It was first class, with fancy lamps and curtains and a woman reading. It didn't look like stopping. Then the brakes screeched. Another carriage passed, then another. The train slowed and stopped with a jerk and a shiver.

I heard a door slam somewhere up the front but I

217

didn't see anyone. I was down the other end, facing right up to a big metal door handle, as if it had stopped there especially for me, my birthday present. I pressed it down. The heavy door opened.

Inside it was dim and damp. Warm air curled round me, pulling me in. I stepped up and closed the door behind me. A second later, the train glided and the station platform fell away.

Thirty-nine

On the Dream Train

I huddled in the corridor, thinking, *If I get caught, that's it.* The time I'd run away on a train before, I'd only got as far as East Croydon, then I'd had to turn myself in because the raving drunk men on the train scared me. Drunken men are prone to lurching around the corridors of trains, it's a fact. But on this train there was nobody. It was just the engine and the hiss of the wheels and the dark shadows running over the floor and walls and ceiling. Maybe I was the only person on the train. Maybe there wasn't a driver, even. Me and the dream train, hurtling off the face of the earth.

Then a man with a baseball cap approached. I froze. You could tell he was Irish, straight off. I remembered from long ago, those early years in Ireland, how the faces on the street were, men lounging on the bridge, women pushing buggies. It felt far off, but the faces were like his and it was home. The man nodded as he walked towards me. His eyes were red. He was no raving drunk, just a fellow needing sleep, same as I did. He broke the spell.

'Is it free?' he said.

I thought he meant the train ride. 'Free?'

'The toilet?' His accent! *Fray*. *Tye-lit*. He pointed and I saw I was standing by a toilet door that said VACANT.

I smiled. 'Yeah. Sure.'

I moved aside and he went in. I went along the way he'd come and stepped over the wonky bit between the carriages. The doors slid apart and I was in a long compartment. There were people scattered, not many. Two murmuring. One snoring. Empty coffee cups. A woman had her arm around a small boy whose head was tucked in her armpit, and even though he was only six or so, he was as Irish as the man I'd just seen. He was sleeping with his mouth open and he had freckles on his nose. His mam was reading and yawning and she shifted, careful so he wouldn't wake. She blew on his hair so the fringe lifted and she smiled, like he was her own private treasure. She didn't see me walk by. She was in a whole other world.

It was like I didn't exist the way nobody looked at me.

Trim used to say how joy-riding the trains is easyville. You dodge the ticket man by moving around, and if you get nervous you lock yourself in the bog. Trim said how he'd been all over England, up to Newcastle where his younger brother was in a foster home, and down to Gravesend where his real dad was and where it's even worse than it sounds, he said. He'd never paid a penny. First you get through the ticket barrier by saying you've been separated from your mum and you pretend to panic. Then you get on the train and do the dodging. Then you get off and say your mum's already gone through the barrier with all the tickets, and you point to a woman who's walking away with a brood of kids. They always believe you, according to Trim. But then you can't trust Trim, Mr I-was-Born-on-an-Aeroplane.

I kept walking, nervous, expecting the ticket man to pounce.

Up the next corridor I saw a man lurking who looked like a guard maybe, so I dashed back the way I'd come. Somebody had opened the window a crack and it was cold. I shivered. Then I saw that the toilet said VACANT again so I locked myself in.

I breathed. I looked in the mirror. Apart from my lipstick mirror, I'd not seen myself in ages.

Do you know what I saw?

It was enough to make a willow weep, big time.

The glamour girl had gone. I looked more like a crackhead who'd just been dragged backwards through a hedge. I was all blotchy cheeks, smudges, hair mish-mashed clumps of blonde and brown and mud stains on my collar. My eyes and nose were red and itching and I'd bitten my lips so much they were bleeding. My hand shook as I got the brush out. I took the wig off. First I brushed my own hair, then I cupped the wig over my fist and brushed it. I washed my face. I took out my toothbrush but realized I had no tooth-paste. I tried to wipe my collar, only the mud smudged. Then I sat on the toilet seat and cried. The tears made my eyes worse, but I couldn't stop.

Miko was beside me like he used to be at the Home when I'd had an almighty smash-up. *Cry all you like, Holly. Because when you stop crying the world will be a different place. A better place. Promise, Holly.*

But this time Miko was wrong. If I stopped crying, nothing would change. The light in the toilet would still be sick-green, and the girl in the mirror sick-green too. She looked at me, and suddenly I saw little Holly again, way back when in the sky house with the falling-down socks and the gold stars from school. A whistle blew and the train swerved and I hung onto the sink edge to stop from falling. *Help*, the girl in the mirror called to me. *Help me. Somebody. Please.* I put a hand out and touched her, and it was as if together we were being dragged back into the sky house, for real this time.

The paint's peeling. A bad smell is coming off the walls. I'm creeping along the hall towards the voices. Mammy and Denny, arguing again. I can hear Mam wailing, 'You spent all our winnings, what more do you want?' Up a level, then down, like the sound of the lifts, but coming from the kitchen. I stand at the door-way. Mam has egg and bacon going in the pan, shaking it round, perched up on the bar stool Denny's got us from a skip. It's like she's too tired to stand. She has her see-through drink in one hand and the spatula in the other, and she's wearing her black dressing gown and her salmon-pink slip and she's scowling.

'I'd rather a liquid dinner,' Denny grumbles, knocking her arm.

'Gerroff,' Mam snaps. 'I've gone and broken the yolk.'

'Can't stand it when the yolk's broke, Bridge.' Denny turns and looks at me. He raises his eyes to heaven. 'She's the worst cook ever to come out of County Cork. Isn't she, H?' That's what he calls me now. Not Doll or Troll, just H. He pronounces it 'Haitch', the Irish way.

'Go brush your teeth, Holl. Scram.' That's Mam speaking. She hands Denny a plate. 'Get away, the pair of you. I've got to iron my blouse.'

Iron my blouse. Iron my blouse. The train speeds up and Mam's words whirl around with the wheels. Then Denny's shouting. *Money. Bitch. Liar. Out.* A clapping sound, a chair falling. I'm in the sky-house bathroom now, hunched up over the sink, and I'm scared. The voices have never been this loud before. Never. I squeeze out the toothpaste but the tube's gone flat and none comes out. So I take it through to Mam again, back up the hall. She's in the lounge now, at the ironing, tottering on her high heels, doing the blouse, the one I like. It's red with yellow embroidery on the collar and cuffs, and on the back there's a dragon and at the front tiny buttons sweep from left to right. She's jabbing the iron round and ignoring Denny, who's still yelling. He stands with the plate askew and the chair's fallen over with its legs in the air and the egg yolk on his plate oozes to the edge.

'Mammy.' They turn and stare at me. 'The tooth-paste's gone.' I hold out the tube.

'Go squeeze it some more,' Mam snaps. Then she

laughs like a madwoman. 'Straighten the old thingamajig out. Go to the bottom, Holl, and work slowly up. Get to it.'

She doubles over and Denny roars like we're in a pantomime.

'Jeez, Bridge,' he wheezes. 'Social services will get you, talking smut to your daughter like that.'

They're shrieking with laughter and I don't know why.

'Get lost, Holl. Bed now,' Mam snorts.

She's telling me to go, so I do. I'm staggering out of the train toilet, back into the corridor. I'm at the open window, breathing the cold air, but I can still hear the voices from the sky house, rising and rising. The train loops and then another one comes *bang* up against us, flying lines of bright metal, and am I dead? No, I'm not. The lights of the other train whisk by, nearer, then further – we're lurching like drunks, and there's Mam's face across the rails in a compartment in the other train. I can see her plainly now. She's looking over my shoulder to something else she's wanting more. And Denny's beside her and they're pointing, wavering, splitting their sides laughing, and the yolk's dripping off the plate and I'm gripping the wig and then the last of the other train goes *swoosh*, and gone, they're all gone.

Forty

Hurry, Hurry, Holly Hogan

The train slowed and the sky house vanished. From somewhere down the corridor a guard's voice called, 'Have your tickets ready please.' I bolted back into the toilet. I stared in the mirror and the face I saw was chalk-white. I ran some hot water and dabbed it on. The reflection misted over and drops of water scuttled down the glass.

'Mammy?' I whispered. 'That wasn't you, was it?'

The train swerved and braked.

My face appeared through the mist, crooked in the water drops.

I got a paper towel and cleaned the mirror. The breeze from the open window had skewed the wig so I put it straight. I saw the amber ring glinting as I smoothed the ash-blonde locks. *Wrong. Mam's face. She's not like that. Not. Cross it out.* I tried to scratch a cross on the mirror with the ring. But it didn't work. Nothing I could do would send that memory-picture of Denny and Mam away to the place where forgotten things belong. I sat on the toilet seat and kneaded the ring.

Take it, Holly. Keep it safe.

My heart slowed down and I breathed. *That* was my mam's voice. Not the other, mocking one. *Safe. Safe.* Somebody fiddled with the toilet door, but I didn't care. Then the train stopped. It was silent. No doors slammed so I knew it wasn't a station, just a stop in the middle of nowhere. I took the amber ring off and stared at the mark it left on my finger. *They'd chop your finger off for a ring like that.* I dropped it back into the front lizard pocket, safe. 'There, Mam,' I whispered, zipping it in. 'It's safe again.'

A voice came over a speaker: '*We will shortly be arriving at Fishguard Harbour. Please ensure you have all your belongings when leaving the train.*' With a groan the train started again. I picked up the lizard, opened the toilet door and looked out. People had gathered in the corridor, standing with cases and backpacks strewn around their feet. I stepped over a holdall to find a free bit of space and put the lizard down. The train speeded up, then slowed, and finally we jerked to a stop on a silent platform.

A man put his arm out the window and released the outside handle. One by one we shuffled out. I was last. The air was cool to the cheek. Somewhere above my head came a mournful cry – a seagull who'd forgotten to go to sleep.

You could smell the sea but you couldn't hear it.

Fishguard, I thought. *Is this real?* I drifted down the platform and nobody stopped me. Along a ramp. Around a corner. Down a corridor. I came to a queue to board the boat. That's where every last one of us was heading. The boat. Every step brought us closer. Soon, I thought. We'll be sailing away into a dream. Soon.

Then I came bang up against a guard checking the tickets. I froze. *Point to a woman with kids ahead of you*, Trim's voice told me. *Say you're with her.* But there wasn't any woman. The woman I'd seen with the small boy sleeping earlier was nowhere. Anyway, I didn't look like a kid myself, not with the wig on. I was too grown up for that trick.

'Ticket?' said the guard.

I looked at him like I didn't understand.

'Your ticket? Where is it?'

I stared at him staring at me and thought, That's it.

'Your ticket, love. I – need – to – see – it,' the guard said like I was stupid.

Slowly I went to get the lizard off my shoulder. Maybe I could just open up all the compartments and pretend how I'd lost the ticket. Maybe – my hand groped my shoulder and the familiar strap wasn't there. The lizard had gone. It wasn't on the ground by my feet. It was nowhere.

'My bag!' I gasped. 'It's gone.'

The guard sighed like he'd seen it all before. 'Did you leave it on the train? Up on the rack, maybe?'

'Must have.' I was shaking.

'Go on. Hurry back, love, before the train pulls out. Quick. We're due to sail.'

I nodded in a frenzy, then turned round and ran back towards the station platform. *Hurry, hurry, Holly*

Hogan. I was running, running and I could see the lizard dangling from the stall on the Broadway and Fiona smiling. *Before the road disappears.* I reached the platform. The train still sat there like a sleeping dragon.

I ran down past the carriages. Which one had I been in? I got to the last but one. That's it, I thought. That's the corridor where I'd left the lizard. That's it—

Then the lights in the carriages went out. *Before you end up falling, falling . . .*

I didn't want to get back on that dark train but I knew I had to. I stepped forward to open the door. But just as I did, the train shuddered, began to move and pulled out of the station, back into the night.

I watched it go, lizard and all. My iPod, my pink-fur purse, my mobile with the charge gone, my SIM card, my lipstick and mirror, my toothbrush, my hair-brush. And in the special zip-up pocket at the front, Mam's amber ring. I was Jane Eyre for sure now. My trunk had gone off with the carriage. I'd lost the jewels. Just like her, I had nothing and nobody left.

Forty-one

The Harbour

I stood for a long time on that platform, with Miko's road-dust song crooning in my head. *Hurry, hurry...* but it was too late.

Dark, alone, no lizard.

Minutes passed, then half an hour. I don't know. Eventually I slipped away, back down the ramp. The guard had gone. I saw a big boat, lit up with tiers of decks, pulling out without me. I might as well have been a ghost, thin and dark and quiet in my trainers. I edged along the walls so nobody would see me. But it was deserted. I didn't know where I was going in the dark. I passed a checkpoint with nobody in it and then lanes with no cars. I followed a path by a roadside and sat on a bit of smooth ground that faced out to sea. Overhead, a half-moon came out, all crooked, like it was ready to tumble out of the sky.

Time went by.

Light crept in.

The sea had no waves. Colours came. Pink, green, red and orange footballs were bobbing in the water. I was back down in Devon with Miko by the harbour front.

'What are they, Miko?' I was asking. 'The things like balls, floating?'

'They're buoys.'

'Boys? Like Trim?'

'No. Buoys. B-U-O-Y-S. They're to tie up your boat.'

I frowned. 'Why don't they float out to sea?'

Miko laughed. 'They're tied down with chains. And an anchor, I guess.'

'A bit like me, Miko.'

'Yeah. A bit like you, a bit like me. Maybe we need those chains, people like us, Holly.'

'Nah, we don't, Miko. We don't need chains. We need freedom.'

The buoys bobbed like mirages on the dark, quiet water. They reminded me of the blood-orange sun hovering over the Welsh hill that I'd seen on the motorbike. Then Grace walked towards me, her hips swinging, turning the pier into a catwalk. I smiled but the picture faded. I stared down at my knees and hugged them because they were warm and real. I drifted.

Daylight got stronger. There were houses on a green cliff and sheds and engine noise. I looked at the ground beneath me. I was sitting on the edge of a mosaic which was labelled:

THE FRENCH INVASION AT FISHGUARD 1797

It showed men and boats and muddled arms, and I was staring at one man hauling another from a boat with a pole. Then I realized he wasn't hauling the man in, but skewering him with a spear.

I stood up, dizzy. In my mind, the spear dripped not with blood, but egg yolk. *Can't stand it when the yolk's broke, Bridge.* I staggered away down the thin strip of causeway like I was drunk.

Holly Hogan, I said to myself. *Get a grip.*

I pinched the skin on my wrist hard.

I got to the end of the causeway and looked out at the sea. Morning came on strong and the sun came up from behind and the sea sparkled.

Holly, keep your nose pointed forward.

Then I saw a dark blob out to sea. And as it got closer, it turned into the boat, returning like an old friend. Gulls wheeled around it. It docked. The harbour came alive. Cars drove off from the hold of the boat. Then new cars arrived, waiting to board. They drove into six long lanes. Most were for cars, but one was for lorries. I stood to the side, watching.

You are off to Ireland under your own steam.

I walked nearer the cars. Seabirds were hopping on the rocks and seaweed. The light was dazzling. Car radios played, posh classical stuff all mixed up with easy listening. Some people got out and picnicked on the harbour-side, or bought drinks, chatted, walked around. Some went to the toilet block. Some stayed in their cars, waiting.

A sign said the boat was sailing again at 9.00.

By 8.15 the lanes were nearly full.

Car doors opened and shut. People kept coming and going.

And that's when I had my plan.

Forty-two

The Hold

So now I'm back to where we started.

I'm breezing down the line of cars so nobody can guess I'm looking for a way to board the boat. I don't care any more if they catch me or not. I'm Miss Devil-Take-a-Running-Jump herself. That's when you're most dangerous, and that was me that morning. Mad, bad Solace. Trim Trouble was nothing compared with me.

Solace whispered in my ear. *Go, Holl. You can do it.*

And when I saw the navy four-by-four, with the mogit coat-flappers yattering down the line and the doors wide open, it was like Fate calling my name. I was in and under the coats before you could say Christmas. When the mogit owners came back they didn't see me. They were too busy arguing about con-ten-gin-seas. Even when the wig slipped off, my luck held and the man at the ticket booth saw nothing either. And then it was clatter-bang up the ramp, and voices, bells, doors slamming, and even though I was under the coats I could feel the low-slung pipes and somewhere hot and deep an engine turning.

But then the owners got out and locked me in. All doors at once. It was like mean steel fingers around my neck, cutting off the air. And soon the boat lurched and we were sailing. Sailing into a bad, dark dream. And the white dividers of the road flew off in all directions and the road dust hit my eyes and the journey went in on itself so that the beginning met the end with the long road falling out from in between, disappearing like Miko warned it would. And the wig had fallen off and I was plain old Holly Hogan and it was the bowels of hell.

Penned in, trapped.

I pounded the window but nobody came.

Let.

Me.

Out.

I was back in the secure unit, the first time they locked me in. I pounded the door then and nobody came. *Cry all you like, sunshine. The door stays shut till morning.* I tore my blankets off the bed, I turned the bed upside down, I lay on the floor and kicked the wall and screamed like my skull would burst. And drawers started opening in my brain, drawers I hadn't opened in years, and I was slamming them shut again but bits of memory kept coming, a voice here, a scream there. I was so scared I was pulling out my own hair. *Please. Let me out.*

The engine rumbled like a beast snarling in its sleep.

Now I gave up the pounding. I was flat out, my

234

cheek against the window, staring at the dim lighting, car on car, lines of bumpers, empty glass, drab colours. I lay back and stared at the green and cream flecks on the ceiling and a big blank hole opened in my head. Darkness rushed in.

Mammy. Where did you go, Mammy? Why did you leave me?

The boat rolled. All around drawers slid open, spilling what was inside, and I couldn't stop them. I didn't want to see, but it was too late, I had. There they were. The three little figurines, Mammy, Denny and little Holly Hogan. We were locked together in the sky house, caught in that moment for all time, like the insect in the amber resin of the ring.

Forty-three

In the Sky House

Sweet dreams are made of this . . . the woman's voice comes from the stereo speakers. Mam's laughing, clamping down the iron on her red embroidered blouse. Denny's laughing too and I'm staring, blinking, wondering why they're mocking me.

'Jeez, Bridge,' Denny yodels. 'Priceless.'

'Scoot, Holl,' Mam says. She brandishes the iron. 'Before I melt your face. Scram.'

I creep out to the bathroom, holding the scrunched-up toothpaste tube. I've got my bottom teeth up over my top lip, biting. I wait. It's silent.

Then.

'Give me the bloody money, Bridge. Give it over.' Denny, roaring. A plate clatters, a knife and fork. I don't want to move but Mammy needs me. My feet are taking me back through to the lounge. The plate's face up on the floor. The egg yolk's set like plastic. The ironing board is over on its side, its steel leg prodding the air. *Who am I to disagree?* goes the song.

'The whore money,' Denny raves. 'I know you've it hidden somewhere.'

It's the money Mam and I are saving to go to Ireland he's talking about. Sometimes Mam puts it in the breakfast cereal. Or in a saucepan in the cupboard. Or down her tall leather boots.

'I've none left,' she snaps. 'None.'

'Liar.'

Now Denny's got her up against the wall, pinned by the shoulders.

'Let Mammy go,' I shout.

Mam's wriggling and shoving. She has the hot iron in her hand and lands it on his arm. Denny howls. 'Liar yourself,' she shouts. 'Thief!'

'Bitch.' He wrenches the iron from her hand and slaps her cheek. 'It's your face I'll melt,' he says. He puts the iron surface up close to her cheek.

They are still. *Everybody's looking for something.*

'Please, Denny. Stop,' Mam whispers.

'I'll melt it, Bridge,' he hisses. 'I'll turn your face to broken yolk. I will.'

'Denny. Please.'

'It's in the boot, Denny,' I squeak.

But I don't exist. He's eyeball to eyeball with her, his hip jutted into her stomach like she's plasticine.

'The money's in Mam's boot,' I yell.

Softly, like it's a kiss, he puts the iron down on her hair so it frizzles, just a little.

'Serves you,' he says. He laughs, steps back. *Sweet dreams are made of this, sweet dreams are made of this . . .* 'Only joking, Bridge.'

She's holding her hair, her mouth open like an O. And Denny's handed her back the iron and he's pushing past me into the bedroom. A boot's being thrown against a wall. Then he's passing back through the lounge and his face is like the mask in the museum, empty and thin, with the dark curls framing it, and his hand's waving. 'Bye, all,' he goes, but he's not looking back.

The front door slams.

'Denny-boy,' Mam whimpers. 'Come back, Denny. Come back.'

But he's gone and I'm glad. He must have used the stairs because there's no sound of the lift whirring.

The Denny figurine's fallen off the edge. One down, two left. Mammy and me.

'Mam?' I'm saying. The music's still playing. She's on her knees, hunched over the toppled ironing board, making sick animal sounds, and her dressing gown's splayed out on the carpet.

I go up and touch her hair. 'Mam?'

'Denny,' she moans.

She looks up and sees me and her eyes go like slits.

'You. 'S your fault, Holl.' She yanks me up close to her face by my pyjama sleeve. She's shaking me. 'Why d'you have to tell him where the money was? You monkey, you. That was my money, mine.'

Now it's me against the wall. And it's the silver flatness and the little holes for steam coming towards me and Mammy's red hand and bony wrist holding it, and I'm kicking her but she's holding me fast with her arm pinned across my neck and I'm biting her and she curses and the iron crash-lands on my head. The smell of the hair is like sparklers after they've died. My head's exploding and the hot metal's on my ear and I'm kicking and screaming and the iron drops hard-bang on my foot. I screech.

'Whisht up, Holl.' She hits me round the face. 'The neighbours will be onto us.'

So my face scrunches up and my shoulders go up and down but no sound comes out.

Me and Mam. Stuck in that moment.

Mam staggers back, shivering.

'Holl,' she whispers. 'You hurt, Holl?'

Now she's got me on the sofa and she's crouched on the floor by my head, putting the red blouse under me like a pillow, and she's more like my own mam again. She's doing it in a dream and her eyes are drifting in and out of focus. 'You all right, Holl?'

'Yes, Mam.'

'You hurt bad?'

'No, Mam.'

'I'm going now, Holl.'

'OK, Mam.'

She crawls over to her bedroom like a baby. She shuts the door behind. I hear a chair fall, a glass break. I hear a drawer being dragged open. Then she comes out, dressed in her best white coat with the grey fur collar. She has her white handbag with the thongs and fringes on her shoulder.

'Gotta run, Holl.' She's shaking like a wind-up toy. 'You stay there on the sofa. I have to find that

Denny-boy and get the money. The money for us, Holl. For us and Ireland.'

'When will you be back, Mam?'

'Soon, Holl. Soo-oo-oon.' She's at the amber ring, pulling it. 'Take this, Holl. Keep it safe. They'd chop your finger off for a ring like that.' She's working it off her finger, pressing it into my palm. 'Keep it safe.' Her words are rattling together like the ice cubes in her see-through drinks.

Her heels are click-clicking away and she's swaying like she's in a ship's corridor as she goes.

'Bye, Mam.'

The front door bangs and the music ends. I hear the lift coming up with its whirring grind. A pause. Then it's falling, taking Mam down, and only the faraway hum of London is left.

'Mammy,' I say. 'Mammy?' But I whisper it quiet, *whisht quiet,* because we don't want the neighbours talking and Mammy will be back soon and she didn't mean to hurt me. I stroke the amber ring and my head is hammering. My foot throbs hot and hard like an engine turning.

Forty-four

Back in the Hold

Mam's heels clicked in my head, going, going, gone. I had my knuckles pressed up to my eyes, like my brain was a blackboard and I was trying to scrub out the pictures on it.

My left foot was under me, throbbing with pins and needles.

I could smell the ship's engines combusting like burned hair.

But the picture of me, the little figurine left over, wouldn't go.

Your fault, Holl. You monkey, you. Scram.

I was the girl on the tiger-skin sofa with the red blouse under her head.

And Mam was looking past me to something else she wanted more.

You can't think all your memories at once or your head will burst. So you put them in a drawer in the back bit of your brain and close them away. Denny and Mam, that day in the sky house, they'd been hidden away for years. And I'd forgotten how the pieces fitted together. I'd fooled myself how it was all Denny's fault and how Mam had to run away from him to Ireland

and how she was waiting for me to find her over there.

It was a dream, I knew that now. The truth was, Mammy burned my hair, then ran away to try to catch Denny, not escape him. The person she'd been running from wasn't him, but me.

Now, in the dim light, I saw what had really happened.

Denny leaving with the money.

Mam with the iron.

And me left over.

The boat sailed on. It was dark and rolling where I was, and I'd found the beginning of my journey, but it wasn't leaving Templeton House or finding the wig. The beginning was in the real sky house, not the pretend one. The last place I wanted to go.

I lay back in the mogits' car and saw the wig on the floor. I picked it up and let it sit on my fist. I'd lost my brush so I ran my fingers through it instead, sorting out the strands.

'Solace,' I whispered. 'Where did you go, Solace? Why did you leave me?'

And I put it on.

Nothing happened. Solace didn't rush into me like a puff of magic air. She didn't laugh or act the clown or blow smoke rings at the world of mogits. She didn't show off her slim-slam hips. She sat there quiet and sad inside me, and she was me and everything we'd done together was me, all me. The nightclub, the thumbing, the backchat, the phoning, the walking, the dreaming, the laughing, the crying. Me on my own. Alone.

Then my own voice sounded out loud in the silent car.

'Oh, Holly.'

Time went by.

Then the boat lurched rougher than before. My stomach somersaulted. I gripped onto the thing next to me and realized it was something I hadn't taken in before.

There's a child seat there, next to you. A child seat, Holl. Remember? A child seat equals a child. And those grey-haired mogits had said something about grandchildren.

Then I remembered how, in the minivan we took down to Devon, Miko put the little ones in the back because there were child locks on the back doors and not on the front. Child locks are there so that children can't fall out. You can only open child-locked doors from the outside, never the inside.

Maybe, I thought, if I tried the front door, it would open. Just maybe.

I was so scared of being disappointed I didn't move.

Go on, Holl. Get to it.

I slunk forward through the seats and wriggled over the handbrake and got to Mrs Mogit's seat. I bit my lip. And I pressed the handle, and did I hold my breath and was my heart pounding . . .

Forty-five

The *Star of Killorglin*

. . . and did the door click open, like magic.

I staggered out, stiff and sore and sick. I breathed.
I closed the door behind me. I couldn't lock it again.
Mr and Mrs Mogit would think they'd forgotten, that
was all. I smelled the oil and metal of the hold and
crept up between the cars, terrified someone would
spot me. But there was nobody. The whole place was
deserted. It was like a multi-storey car park on the
move.

I found a door with a sign saying TO UPPER DECKS. I
opened it and stepped over the bit at the bottom that
looked like its only purpose was to bash your shin. On
the other side was a staircase. I climbed the steps, up
and up.

Then I was walking through lounges and past fruit
machines, and all the talk buzzed in my ears. Daylight
came through the portholes but you couldn't see
much for the thickness of the glass. People were sleeping on chairs, drinking from plastic cups. In a corner
I spotted Mr and Mrs Mogit. She was reading a

magazine with a frown on her face. 'Just you listen to this,' Mrs Mogit said. 'It's shocking.' But I didn't wait to hear. I drifted past them and up the steps and down a corridor and past the portholes. A man lurched past me as if the boat was in a storm but it wasn't, he was drunk. Flat-out. His cheeks were red and his eyes dim and I knew he had a blank hole inside him, like I had, and maybe that's what it had been like inside Mam, and Denny too.

I passed another row of fruit machines with nobody playing them, only a small boy. I paused to watch him. He was only just big enough to reach the lever. When no money came out, he kicked the machine and his face turned to crazy paving.

'Hey, boy,' I said. 'Cheer up. Have this.'

I'd remembered the last of Phil's money, stashed in my skater-top pocket. I held the coins out to him. The little boy squinted up like I was a freak.

I smiled. 'Go on. Take them. I don't want them.'

He reminded me of the little ones at the Home. They didn't trust you as far as they could throw you. Slowly his hand came out and took the coins. When he spoke, it was in the strongest accent I'd ever heard.

'That yoke. 'S bad.'

'The fruit machine?'

'Yus. 'S false.'

'Try the next one up.'

He shuffled up. I waited to see how he'd do, but he glared round to let me know I was putting him off. I took a step back and put my two hands together like a prayer and he smiled. Then he pulled and a good

245

trickle of money came down the shoot. He yelped and hee-hawed like an insane donkey.

'Nice one,' I said.

'D'you want a cut?' he asked, only it sounded like *coort*.

'Nah. It's yours.'

'Sure?' He held out a ten-pence piece.

'Certain.' I remembered Junior Einstein in the museum with his aliens and meteorites. How would it be if those two boys changed places in the world? I wondered.

'Sure you're sure?'

'You keep it. Have another go.'

He tried but nothing happened so he kicked the machine and went back to the first machine and put another coin in and this time he got another trickle back.

'You're one lucky boy,' I told him. 'What's your name?'

'Joseph Ward. What's yours?'

'Holly Hogan.' I smiled.

'Me da's sister's a Hogan,' he said.

'Oh, yeah?'

'Maybe you's a Traveller too?'

'Yeah, sure I am,' I said. 'I travel the world and the seven seas.'

He frowned. 'This is the *Irish* Sea.'

'It counts, I guess. Where are you headed?'

'Dunno. We get off the boat and drive and Da gets a lay-by and there's home and Mam makes the tea.'

'Oh.'

246

'An' I'm on my holidays and I'm not going to school. Not ever. Da says.'

'You *are* lucky.'

'Where're you going?' he said.

'Home too.'

He grinned. 'D'you want a go?' he said, holding out another coin.

'Nah.' Then I remembered how the Irish say good-bye. 'Good luck.'

'Good luck,' he said and turned back to the slot machine.

I walked away, cash-free.

I pushed a door open against a hard wind.

Right away I had to grab onto the wig to stop it flying. I walked out onto the open decks. There were life buoys, red and white, and on them was written THE STAR OF KILLORGLIN, which was how I knew the name of the boat.

One side of the deck was windy and the other still. Everyone sat on the still side, so I stayed on the windy side. I kept one hand on the wig. The boat slapped up against the waves. Another drawer slid open in my brain. It was me at the Kavanaghs' house, waking up early after a bad dream, and seeing Mam in the picture I kept by my bed. Her lips were parted and her eyes slanted off to one side. Her hair blew off from her cheeks and she tilted her face like the wind was a lover. And that's how it was. She was always looking past me like I didn't count, filing her nails, doing her foundation, trying on her new shoes, choosing her bag, and telling me to scram. She was always going, with the lift fading away to silence and me being left alone.

And that morning at the Kavanaghs', I remembered the real Mam in the real sky house. The lips that didn't smile, ripped. The eyes like slits, ripped. The bits of paper falling on the bedcover. Then I'd slept again. When I woke and found the bits torn up it was like someone else had done it, in someone else's dream.

I looked out to sea. The ocean was beautiful, white, bright water and cream foam, like it'd come to boiling point. It was cold and true like my memory and hard and clear like my choice.

Chloe on the coach to Oxford smiled at me. *Thule was sighted, but only from afar. A place where you always wish you could go.*

There was land ahead, dark purple, like a bruise. Ireland. I smiled because now I knew what Chloe meant and I hadn't understood before.

Grace's gentle eyes stared up at me from the foam. Trim was laughing like he'd never stop. I don't believe in modern-day miracles, I said to the writer man who came to our school that time. Maybe they happen to other people, but not to me.

I remembered now the long waiting in the sky house after Mam ran off. How night came and I turned on all the lights. How morning came and I didn't go to school because I knew I had to stay and wait. Me and the walls and the silence, quiet. I crept around like I was nobody so as not to disturb the neighbours.

I went into Mam's bedroom and sat at her dressing table and saw my ear blistered and my hair mangled and burned. I got the scissors and cut off the burned hair in hunks, close to the scalp. Then I played with Mam's lipsticks and in a drawer found the picture of her on the beach and put it with the amber ring she'd given me and kept them safe.

And had my Krispies fizzed up in Coke, because the milk was off.

And played Snap by myself with my animal card pack, only half the cards were missing.

I don't know how long I was in the sky house on my own, waiting. But sometime a doorbell rang, and then there was knocking and a woman calling my name through the letterbox. I hid under my bed with the ring and the picture. I remember the dust and the old shoes and the hard prickle of carpet. Then somebody pulling me out by the arms, out of the sky house for ever.

The boat crept closer towards the coast. My dream shattered. The cows wandering over the green hill, the dogs on their bellies laughing, a dream. Mammy smiling a welcome in her halter-neck dress, a dream. The soft pints of air, a dream. The rain like silk, a dream.

Miko had my bulging file in his hand. *She left you, Holly. And how does that feel?*

He gave me one last look and turned away.

Fiona was gazing sadly at me in my bedroom at Templeton House the first time we met. I wasn't the child she'd wanted but someone else.

Ray was looking at the sky and the letters H – O – L – L – Y were drifting apart, vanishing like they'd never been.

I crouched down out of the wind and unlaced my trainers.

Miko, Grace, Trim, Fiona, Ray. Going, gone, clean out of my life. Only it was me leaving them now, not them leaving me.

The sun slanted down from a cloud and the waves danced.

Go girl, Solace whispered. *You and me, for ever.*

My throat was sore like it'd forgotten how to swallow.

Don't be afraid, girl. Go.

I stepped out of the trainers.

Before you change your mind. Quick.

I clung to the edge as the boat ran smooth. Below was a trail of foam, bubbling and playing all the way back to England. There was light on the water. *You can meet God on the road, Holly. God on the road, God on the road.* Phil was driving his truck through the top of the forest and looking down on the wide Severn. *Do it.* Voices from the past, the good and the bad, the ones who cared and the ones who didn't. The girl on the *Titanic* was laughing, her hair swept up by the wind, a goddess leading the way.

Now, girl. Jump.

There was shouting and laughing and tugging and pulling. The squares on the dance floor flashed. Bodies twisted and came together and parted again.

Somebody's arms swooped past me. The Solace in me screamed, hard and fierce. Go! The boat lunged, the wave slapped. My ash-blonde locks streamed upwards and outwards, as if they were reaching for the sky.

Forty-six

Solace Soars

But something happened before I jumped. A squall of wind hit me and the wig blew off. I tried to catch it but it went too fast. It skimmed overboard and danced in the air, its locks looping like kite tails. It soared up and the strands spun silver like a Catherine wheel, as if the invisible person wearing it was spinning for joy. Then it swooped down and away from me. My own hair rippled over my face, brown and fierce, and Fiona's voice came strong in my head. *My hair grew back, Holly. Only differently.* I touched the thin brown strands and they were mine. They were strong and straight and the smell of the burning had gone.

The wig dropped with a final flash of blonde into the creamy foam and vanished.

And I didn't hurry after it. I stopped right there.

It was as if Fiona was reaching for my shoulder. She was walking down the Broadway Market, calling, coming towards me, not walking away. And the shoppers turned round and called me too, and there

in the middle was Miko, tall as a door, shouting, *Wait, wait, Holly Hogan. Wait.*

And so the wig that had reminded Fiona of a bad, sick time was washed far away into the white water. Maybe it floated out to the open ocean and it's travelling the seven seas. Or maybe it sank and drifted to the bottom and fishes are swimming through those ash-blonde strands and it's crusted over with shells. Or maybe it reached Ireland. Maybe it washed up on the beach with the wood and the seaweed and it's rocking there on the sand with the tides. And a seagull has plucked out its hairs for her nest and plump feathery baby birds are keeping it warm and dry.

I don't know.

But Solace was gone, and Holly Hogan, aged fifteen years and one day, was back.

Forty-seven

Thule

I turned away from the railing of the boat and padded down the deck in my bare feet. I forgot to put my trainers back on. To the front, the indistinct horizon had unfurled into rocks and hills and fields, dabs of pink and grey. Rosslare harbour appeared. There was a green hill with cows walking over it and the water was blue and there was a ribbon of road, skirting the cliff, shining, and it was Ireland, lit soft as a dream.

But I didn't join the queue to disembark. I didn't go down to the hold to find a ride. I stood on the deck, looking at the dock and the people and the cars. I breathed the Irish air.

Then I turned from the railing and found the purser's office, where a uniformed man and woman were chatting. I went in and told how I was a stowaway and they laughed like I was making it up. But I didn't laugh back. I couldn't even speak. Then they saw I didn't have any shoes and I must have looked wild and filthy, because they stopped laughing. The man asked who I was and where was my mum. I said my name,

Holly Hogan, and my age, fifteen and one day, and then how I had no mum and how Fiona and Ray were fostering me at 22 Mercutia Road, London.

They said for me to stay on board and sat me in a room with a tiny porthole. The woman brought me a Coke and fish and chips and I gobbled them down. Then I had to go to the bathroom to throw them up again. They sailed me back to Britain and I never even set a toe on Irish soil. I was like the Roman guy who sailed past Thule and didn't have time to stop. And maybe I was sad or maybe not, because one day I'd sail there again.

They took me back through Wales and England in a car. I don't remember much of the ride. I looked out the window but we went by motorway and there wasn't much to see, so I fell asleep.

Forty-eight

Road Dust

They didn't send me to the secure unit. Instead they took me to a hospital on a hill in south London for people who have mental problems. And when I saw the sign I nearly did go mental, but a nurse came and said how it would be OK because I'd only be there a short time and being there didn't mean you were mad and I didn't have to worry about syringes or strait-jackets, and the other people in my ward were just like me, tired and unhappy and needing to talk things over.

And it was OK. They didn't lock you in and the windows were big with sunshine coming through.

They sent a lady psychologist to see me every day. She sounded a bit like the Gayle woman from the care-babe phoneline, but her name was Mrs Rajit and she was Indian. We sat and chatted about things we liked and didn't like. Colours, numbers, food. Then I told her about the road and the white dividers and how in the end I'd reached the sky house and what I'd found there.

I told her about how I'd nearly jumped.

'Why did you take your trainers off, Holly?' she asked me.

'Dunno. Just did.'

'Were you planning on jumping?'

'Yeah. Guess.'

'Were you planning on dying?'

'Yeah. S'pose. I mean, why jump otherwise? You don't jump off a big ship like that just for a quick dip, do you?'

'So why did you take your trainers off?'

She finished me, Mrs Rajit. 'Dunno. Like I said.'

But I knew what she was after, so then I said how I wanted to jump but I wanted to swim too. Maybe with my trainers off, I'd have had a chance to live. Maybe another boat would have come and picked me up. But since I didn't jump, why ask? And Mrs Rajit smiled and moved on to the next question.

Then Fiona, question-queen herself, was allowed in to see me. I was scared stiff she'd be livid and I trembled as she walked down the aisle of beds.

'Oh, Holly,' was all she said when she saw me. 'Holly.'

She sat on the bed and her eyes filled and I was the last whale harpooned, official.

She said how Ray and she had been up the wall and down again and how she'd taken to making a patchwork quilt with the worry, which was some joke because she was useless at sewing. And all the time she was stitching the squares together she was thinking, what had she done wrong to make me run? I bit my lip and said about the wig and how the wig and me turned into a mad, bad girl called Solace and how I'd hit the road and chased the white dividers all the way to Wales and how I thought I'd find my mam in Ireland. Then I told her about the iron and Mam burning my hair and all the other things I'd found in the real sky house.

'Oh, Holly,' she whispered. 'You do remember.'

Then she came in every evening, and Ray too.

Fiona got me grapes and magazines and slices of pizza, which you were allowed to microwave in the kitchen. And Ray bought me an iPod to replace the one I'd lost, loaded with my favourite Storm Alert songs plus a new weirdo band he'd got into called String Theory.

Then one day, Fiona brought me in my file. It was my right to see my file and I said I wanted to have my right. The police report said how Mammy was on the Game and a User and how Denny Supplied and was a User too. The social services were on to her and had put me on something called a Child Protection Register. Then Mam did a runner and went back to Ireland and disappeared. Only she'd rung social services before she left and said how I was in the flat and would they take me. And the file said how they'd found me with my burned, chopped hair and my ear blistered and foot swollen and how I didn't talk, only to say 'Where's Mam?' so I knew my memory had come back straight and true.

It was in the file and in my head, only I'd kept it shut away.

If she were me, Fiona said, she'd be livid and want to nuke the whole world to get back at that person who was supposed to love you but had gone clean out of your life like that. The thought of Fiona with her save-the-whale eyes nuking the world made me smile.

Ray got the job up north but turned it down. He told Fiona and me how he wanted to go into cruise-mode with his work and ditch the overtime at weekends and take up the bass guitar. At the case conference he stood up for me. He said I'd been good in the house and given up smoking without even being asked and all three of us wanted to try again. Fiona nodded and cried and I stared at my hands and wished I could have a fag. But they believed Ray and said OK.

So it was back to 22 Mercutia Road. When I came out of hospital, Ray and Fiona told me how as a surprise birthday present they'd arranged for me to have a dog. That was why Fiona was going to be late the day I ran away. She was going to the kennels to make the arrangements. We had to wait until he was eight weeks old before he could leave his litter, then he came home with us.

Now we've had him over a year and he's one mad eejit, as Miko would say. He's the kind that's like a stretched limousine, the way his belly rubs along the floor, his front and back legs are so far apart. I didn't call him Rosabel because he's a he. His name is Thule, like the place you dream about. But we often call him Fool, and sometimes Drool because that's what he does.

I went back to school and Karuna and I became mates, official. And sometimes we let mad Max the bell-ringer hang out with us because he's even more certifiable than we are. Karuna's gone from being a townie to a goth and, no kidding, she's making her own coffin in woodwork. Mrs Atkins made me write a long story about how Jane Eyre marries Mr Rochester under false pretences and how it is when she finds out on honeymoon on the French Riviera that he's married already and he's tricked her. I made up how she's furious and steals a rowing boat to escape back to England but is picked up by pirates instead. So she decides to be a pirate too and all the men pirates are in love with her and she rules the roost. And her name is Janie Jewel the Cruel, on account of all the gems she steals. And it was better than the real *Jane Eyre* any day. Mrs Atkins gave me A-minus and read it out to the class and Karuna never lets me forget it.

I still see Mrs Rajit once a week. Sometimes the words don't come, so instead I draw her pictures of the sky house. Other times I tell her about everyone I met on my travels. I show her the map and describe the good people on it who were like guardian angels because they did something to help me and asked for nothing back.

Chloe, who told me about Thule.

Kim, who gave me a sandwich.

The magnet man.

The boy on the motorbike whose name I never knew, and Kirk, even, with his truckload of pigs.

Sian, who said I had a figure like a dancer.

And Phil with his sad vegan eyes giving me the cake with pretend candles, and God is sitting in him still, I bet you, and he's taking the scenic routes and chasing the white dividers in his cheese truck, planning his next move.

As for the Templeton House crew, I never saw them again. I still hear Miko's voice in my head sometimes. And I see him smiling, looking down at me from the top of a hill, his guitar slung over his back. I hope he's doing all right. Rachel told me Trim went straight from care into young offending, smooth as an arrow, so he never got the chance to start up his casinos. And Grace left the Home and wouldn't say where to. So I buy the magazines and I look out for her supermodel face. There are pretty girls in there, all colours of skin. Sometimes there's one with caramel cheeks and hair in braids and for a second I have to look twice. But whoever it is isn't a patch on Grace, with her eyes shining like dark coins and her as-if smile. But I keep looking and hoping how one day I'll find her, walking down a catwalk, wearing jewels and spangles, just like she dreamed. *It's like walking to the sky, Holly,* she's calling from the centre page. *Walking up to heaven, Holly, without having to die first.*

Acknowledgements

Many thanks to the social workers I met in Oxford at the child rights training course in 2004. The stories about their work were inspirational. Pete Treadwell in particular put me straight on a number of things in the realm of children 'who are being looked after'. I'd also like to thank ChildLine and the Who Cares? Trust, whose publications were invaluable.

Fiona Dunbar, Oona Emerson, Helen Graves, Sophie Nelson, Alison Ritchie, Linda Sargeant, Anna Theis and Lee Weatherly were also most helpful in various ways. And words can hardly express the debt I owe to my agent Hilary Delamere and my quintet of editors, Annie Eaton, Kelly Hurst, Bella Pearson, Ben Sharpe and, in particular, David Fickling. The journey was winding but they never flagged.

Finally, thanks to Geoff for driving me up and down a certain old trunk road by way of research. It was a sky-jump, as Holly would say.

I have added the names of Helen Graves, Sophie Nelson and Alison Ritchie to this list because I know Siobhan would have wanted me to.

DF

Copyright Acknowledgements